# Chase Robinson

## By David W. Smith

For Pat, who would have loved all of this.

# Chapter One

## I Wish She Had Horns

It's hard to trust someone when you know that they're killing people. Having said that, who's killing who - and why - are likely relevant questions in the whole trust equation. In my life, it's been my mother doing the killing.

That probably makes things worse.

Not that I know for sure, because I don't have a mother who doesn't kill people, so I don't know what that's like.

It's not the sort of calculation I thought I'd ever have to make - weigh all the reasons I should trust her, all the risks she's taken for me, all the things she's done for me my whole life against what I can only call a body count.

I had no clue about any of it until three of my friends gave me the bad news. Not about the killing. Worse. Carter, who must have drawn the short straw, told me. "Chase," he said gravely, "your mom is hot."

"What?"

It caught me off guard. I have very little insight into how my mother actually appears to other people. To me, she looks like herself.

"You know, older than us, but hot, like Cate Blanchett in *Thor: Ragnarök*," Rich explained. "When she has hair and not horns."

"Yeah, the horns were creepy," Carter agreed. "Talk about dark roots."

Their comments came after I had complained loudly and colourfully about the men Mom dates. There seemed to be a lot of them all of a sudden. It was awful.

We were at a decision point during lunch break at school - about to choose between homemade salt and fat to the left and store-bought salt and fat if we kept going straight. My mom and her alleged hotness had come up as I mentioned that her busy social life meant there wasn't much to eat at my place just now.

"No - stop it." Amy rolled her eyes. "Chase's mom is just *well-put-together.*"

I guess that's a better way of saying it even if I'm not sure what it means. I just looked at the three of them, probably with an open mouth. They interpreted my silence as emotional turmoil and took me straight to Aladdin's Middle-Eastern Café to fill my gaping maw with hot cheese-stuffed flatbread.

So gimme a break. Of all the barriers I had anticipated to the hassle-free operation of The Plan - that's the plan of my life going forward from, like, NOW - I had not expected this sort of setback. Lack of money, failing grades, a tornado obliterating our home, these things I had considered because they had all happened to other people I knew.

But a mother who is out there? And hot?

Who has one of those?

It was and is weird. It's not like I had any experience to rely on, that I'd had a series of mothers who dated men all over the place and I was all cool with it and understood the needs of an empowered twenty-first-century professional woman.

I don't want to know about her needs. Not those ones. I admitted as much to Amy between bites of burning cheese pie and she called me selfish and immature.

I'm sure she's right. So hate me on Twitter.

But try to understand there were other issues as well. Because not every hot mom turns out to be a killer. That might make for a lot of killers, given that there appear to be hordes of men out there who don't consider motherhood an immediate turn-off.

To account for the killing, though, there has to be a bunch of things going on, a combination of factors.

Me, my existence, my presence was probably one.

Wait. Not probably.

Definitely.

So it didn't matter that I was not the one piling corpses like firewood. Because whatever was going to happen, however big the stack of bodies became, it would be my fault - just because I was there. Or here, I guess. Being *my* mother made her into a killer. But being a killer means that I am having a hard time trusting my mother to make good decisions about herself and her life, let alone me and mine.

That sucks, and because I cannot conceive of a universe in which I do not exist, there's nothing I can do about it.

I cannot be unborn.

She cannot unkill people.

And I think maybe she trusts me even less than I trust her.

# Chapter Two
## The Relationship Gap

Responsibility and fault are different planets, a lot like killing and murder. It is not my fault that I was born. It was not my mother's fault either, although you could argue that it was her responsibility.

And there are many levels to my responsibility that evolved long after my babyhood. Like now, in my late teenagehood. Mom thinks *she* needs to be *with* someone. Someone not me. Big surprise, I don't do it for her, being her awkward kind of underdeveloped seventeen-year-old son, with a surname from a father long gone.

I never really considered that Mom wanted to replace He-Who-Ran-Away-From-Us, to fill a relationship gap in her life, and if I had, I'd have imagined it differently. My future-focused family might include some rich older dude who would slide in and give Mom all his money just to be his overpaid personal medic. He'd let me drive his collection of classic British sports cars and insist that we accompany him on trips to Thailand and Guadeloupe. She'd look after his gout while I went body-surfing. And there would be no hint, no possibility of anything cringy happening between them.

I told my friends that, and Carter and Rich nodded their heads in understanding. Amy didn't get it at all. Under her carefully beat-up New York Yankees hat, her eyebrows furrowed over her devastating green eyes. She looked at me as if to say, *what?*

As if I was the one who didn't make sense. She doesn't even *like* baseball.

Choosing men to date was probably hard for Mom. I suppose she was out of practice. She raised me by herself, rarely socialized, just took care of business. Because we had no relatives in town and we didn't have any money, she had to wait until I was old enough to be left alone, which I had been for years now, so I think it took some time for her decision to, you know, get out there.

And then when she did there seemed to be something wrong with all the guys. I know I sound like a forty-year-old single woman who's been on too many of *those* dates, but all the good men seem to be taken. All the nice single guys seemed to be gay, and while that solved a problem for me, Mom considered a romantic relationship with a gay man a non-starter.

The guys she did date seemed to be younger or older or weirder than they should have been. And losers. Why were they all losers?

Don't worry - no one was going to get killed just for being a loser. The death toll would be staggering and the power vacuum at the top level of elected government and at Facebook might be difficult to fill.

One of the first losers was Ed Taggart. Real estate is his passion. That's what it says on all of his signs and that's what he says when you first meet him. Big smiling face on all the bus stop benches. I think he was looking for arm candy to go to open houses with him, show people in, offer them cucumber water. A car-show model to smile and bask in his glow. Mom wasn't keen. But at least the Edster didn't look at us like we were beneath him.

Ralf Griffiths did. Flashy black Acura, skinny suit and tie, manicure to match his toothy smile and a part in his hair that would cut steel. Glanced around our house like it amused him. He was a total dick, into himself as a way of life. Him, I wanted to punch. Not kill, because he needed to live with the fact that a skinny seventeen-year-old could kick his ass.

Randy Worsley was a ball of energetic anxiety, fidgeting, laughing, starting sentences but never finishing them, making most of them into questions. "Maybe we should ...? I hope I'm not being too ...? What is that, a ...?"

He managed a bulk food co-op. Smelled like olives. I wanted to throw up when I stood next to him. I think Mom did, too. We maybe felt a little sorry for Randy. No killing potential there.

But losers. Inadequate, neurotic, arrested, needy, occasionally narcissistic, at times borderline pathological personalities. All of them.

But she's hot, so they are also intensely interested in my mother.

Of course, they didn't know she's a killer. Or was a killer. Or soon would be. It's complicated.

# Chapter Three

## The GareBear

Do sociopaths know they're sociopaths? That might be something I'd ask Google, but I have to be careful what I put into my search history these days. It's one of the inconveniences associated with the new state of things. And there are a lot of those.

Do I sleep at night because I am a sociopath or because I am not? The idea that killing and murder are different lets me sleep, but maybe that's just a convenient rationalization. My way of dealing with my sense of responsibility.

So, here's another of the ways I am accountable for my mother's killing issues.

I failed to act soon enough. Because I trusted her too much.

I didn't think he was anyone to worry about. It seemed pretty obvious that she could do better than Gary Two-Step, so I figured he was a temporary distraction at most. His real name was Twolan, but I call him Two-Step because he thought he was a good dancer, which he told me the first time I met him, like it would impress me. He had nice teeth, all of his hair and a knock-off assembly-line personality. I thought he would be a brief, uncomplicated joke. I didn't take him seriously.

My bad. The Plan, the one that I developed for my future, was in mortal danger. Turns out Gary was, too, not that I understood that at the time. What was clear to me at the beginning was that I miscalculated the effect of his smile, and his lame jokes and the sheer weight of all the shared time he and Mom spent together. Thinking back on it, that much Gary was sure to set just about anyone down the road to killing.

Not to say that Gary wasn't clever in his way. He spent money on things Mom liked, like concerts, theatre, and nights at comedy clubs. He was deferential and accommodating, seeing her whenever she could fit him in, as if she were the only person in the world that mattered to him. He was understanding of her odd hours, interested in everything she said, and tolerant of her weenie teenage son.

Mom was happy, she was enjoying her hours away from work and from home. Everything subtly changed one day after she'd had a particularly late night out with Gary. Mom rarely drinks at all, saying that alcohol makes her say stupid things, but I think she might have that night. She had a day off, and I am not high-maintenance so she could afford to sleep in, drink coffee and enjoy walking Loki the Ill-Bred Mutt. Then Gary showed up in the late afternoon.

She was tentative with GareBear when he came over, while he looked really pleased with himself, relaxed and in control. I had to leave to do a shift at the store, so I wasn't around for their conversation. But when I got back, when I talked to her the next day, everything had changed and none of it made sense. It was a grey late spring afternoon when Mom told me, while pretending to ask me, that he was moving in.

"It's ... temporary, Robinson," she said. "He lost his apartment and now he needs a place to live while he gets back on his feet. He'll sleep in the spare room, so you need to take your things out of there." She always uses my last name when she's serious and the pause often precedes bad news. And this was the kind of bad news I had never experienced before. Thinking of Gary Two-Step living in my house was a trauma, a life-concussion, the feeling that I was about to undergo immediate yet medically unjustifiable surgery.

And Mom's attitude was impossible to figure out. She was clearly less than happy with the situation, far less happy than she was when they had started to date. If she was in love with this guy, why wasn't she happy? Why was he moving into the spare room? If she wasn't in love with this guy, why would she let him move in at all?

How does a grown man "lose" an apartment? He doesn't - he gets kicked out. Probably because he has no money. And this is someone we want living with us? You can't blame me if I started to have trust issues with my own mother. She was bringing this unwanted blight into my life and I could not understand why. How do you trust someone who doesn't make sense?

I was speechless with questions, but Mom was so clearly closed to all discussion of it that I kept them to myself. He arrived and sections of my life were lopped off with horrifying rapidity.

My privacy. My peace and quiet. My psychological space.

Gone.

Not for a couple of days or even a couple of weeks. It stretched and lengthened and lasted and persisted, every minute a bad dream that wouldn't end. And that's the way I walked through it - in a surreal fog, a daze of disbelief as I expected the dream to end, things to improve, change by themselves, the same miracle of life as spring following winter.

But there was no spring, just the summer from hell as Gary's assprint got bigger and bigger, as his body odour got pukier, as his attempts to get along with me got fewer and ever more pathetic.

His idea of male bonding was to give me dating advice.

"Smart guys know how women like to be talked to, you know?" He winked at me. When I didn't ask for more information he gave it to me anyway. "Tell them what they want to hear, but do it by listening, be fascinated by their stories - about their day or their lives, it doesn't matter. You'll score every time." It was as if my mother, the woman he'd been seeing, wasn't in the next room and wasn't my MOTHER.

It quickly became clear to me why he was so accommodating when they were dating. He didn't actually have a job or any prospect of a job, or any desire to get one, seeing that things were working out so well for him. GareBear put on a show for a while, pretended to care about contributing to the family unit. He paid cash for his own beer, which seemed to be his primary expense other than gas for the Garemobile. I don't know how he got the money he had, and I never found a credit card when I looked through his stuff.

If he got the sense that either Mom or I were annoyed with his burping, farting, overly loud laughter or all-around sloth, he'd just smile and say, "I'm a natural person. I have a big personality." It was the kind of personality that liked to go out in the middle of the night, sometimes twice. I would always hope, almost pray except that I don't, that his natural self would get lost in the dark, that he wouldn't return.

But he did. And it sucked.

He had a lot of valuable advice, though, when he was through complaining about the quality of the accommodation. We properly needed a whole new heating system, and some chairs with better lumbar support, said the G-Bear. I suggested that his back might feel better if he picked his ass off the couch from time to time, but he took exception.

"You are lucky I'm here, kid. I'm all that's standing between you and complete disaster."

Disaster? Early the next morning I got up to talk to Mom while she was getting ready to head off to work. Not much chance of smelling the GareBear before eleven, so I thought we could talk. I asked her what he meant by that - the complete disaster - and she just said that I should, "Stay out of his way." That just made me mad.

"Have you ever considered that he's the one who's in MY way?" I complained.

"Yes, of course - but you're not the dangerous one."

"Does that mean HE is? Then what the hell ..."

She stopped me with one hand opening the door and the other on my chest. "I will look after this. Stay away from him and let me do what I have to do." I couldn't argue as the door closed in my face and she was off to catch her bus.

It didn't seem like she was looking after much one night when she came home from a late shift and found him in her bed. She tried to keep her voice down, but he didn't. I was awake texting Amy about how much I hated my life, so I heard the whole thing.

"Come on, Kelly! Relax! You knew this was gonna happen someday."

"No, it isn't - not now, not ever." Her voice had that clenched-teeth edge to it that happens when you're trying not to shout but you're totally pissed off.

"I wouldn't be too sure. Remember - there are certain things that you may have to do if I'm gonna keep my mouth shut."

I heard a door slam and lock after that. I assume it was Mom's. I lay in my own room for a while curled up on my bed, my hands balled into fists, trying to control the rage I felt. That phrase, the one about *having* to do ... something was going through my brain. Mom had used it, and Gary just had too. I am not one for violent thoughts, but that night a number of scenarios went through my head that involved a lot of disturbing images. But every time I thought about how satisfying it would be to whack Gary on the head or stick him with something sharp, my mind would follow with the logical consequences. Jail or a vendetta proclaimed by Gary's loser allies. Or both.

I spent a lot of time there - in my room - with noise-cancelling earphones for protection. If I didn't see his face or hear his farts, then I could pretend that he didn't exist, that he was not in my home, leeching off of my mother, spending endless hours talking in a moderate bellow on the phone. I put off going home, staying at work or even at the library until they practically threw me out. I met my friends at their places or at the mall or anywhere Gary did not naturally inhabit.

Amy came to get me one day and had to put up with the GareBear looking her up and down like she was a shiny new car. That's when I understood what that expression means - objectifying someone. That's what he did.

"We should all go out together," he said to Amy as we left, as if I wasn't even there. "Get to know you better." And he stroked her upper arm with the backs of his fingers.

I got us out as fast as I could. We walked away, headed for the bus to go to a movie. "Really sorry about that, about him. Sorry that he ... exists. I hate him."

"Yeah, well, it makes me wonder why your mom doesn't see through him," she said.

"It's weird - I can tell that she knows he's a dick, but she refuses to talk to me about him or why he's there. I don't think he's paying rent. She steps away every time he tries to touch her, which he does a lot because he's such a natural person. And it gets worse."

"What do you mean?"

"He's pressuring her to move IN move in. Into her room. With her. The thought of being there, him in bed with my mother is making me physically ill. Seriously, I'm swallowing puke."

"What does *she* think?"

"Her exact words were, 'not now, not ever.' He's not liking getting no for an answer - it's easy to tell. You should see his eyes. Intense."

"Is he threatening her?"

"His existence is an implied threat, but other than that she won't tell me. Like she can't trust me, like she thinks I can't handle it."

"It's not about you. For some reason, your mom doesn't think she can get rid of him. He has some hold over her. Either you have to find out what's holding her back, or ...."

"Or what?"

She had a hard edge in her voice. "Or you need to *do* something about him."

"Do what?"

"Do your thing. Get creative."

As we made our way to the multiplex that one word stayed with me. Creative. I could do that.

# Chapter Four

## Mysteries of the Creative Process

$A$my's comment made me realize that my creativity had been kept in check, even stifled by GareBear's presence. I felt a need to express myself and Amy's suggestion about doing something creative about GareBear gave me moral authority.

Or compromised me completely. Don't care which.

Deceit and guile are just other terms for scriptwriting. Mom did not trust me enough to share whatever Gary had over her, so I saw no reason to consult her. I developed an independent strategy to rid my life of the hairball that walks like a man.

How hard could it be? Given that he was stupid and useless, and I am not, I was sure I could provide Gary with the motivation necessary to move out on his own. I introduced the normal clutter that goes along with moving in with your friend and her teenage son. If GareBear could freely express his true self in our home, then so could I.

I just dialed my behaviour back to the way I lived before I realized what a pain in the ass I was for Mom. Simple acts of omission came first, the kind of thing you do when you live alone, which I did a lot simply because Mom worked long hours. I made sure my feet were nice and ripe in my runners before taking them off so that something in the house always smelled worse than Gary did. I left my backpack where he'd trip over it, made sure to put an empty roll in the toilet paper dispenser whenever I could, hung wet towels on his chair.

I got used to his routine and made short expeditions into the room he never paid rent on. The first time I almost passed out on the stink of cheap body wash and aftershave. But I was able to take stock of his personal effects and their locations. Later, I started stealing. Like a hairbrush or eye drops, so he thought he'd mislaid them. I'd return them to slightly different locations, but not until he bought replacements.

Because he made rewarding sounds when he was angry and frustrated, I experimented with locks, drawers, his phone cover, the case for his reading glasses. I discovered these things can be closed with tiny, invisible amounts of superglue. All the while I made sure his keys and wallet were never where he left them.

And peanut butter. When I was told that GareBear was seriously allergic - like call-the-paramedics allergic - I would pretend to try to clean it up but always leave an obvious spot of oil here and there, just to keep him on his toes.

"What is your problem? How stupid are you?" he'd say when he thought he'd found peanut oil. "I'm telling you I could stop breathing!"

"I'm sure I could jab you with your EpiPen. You do have one, right? Somewhere?"

"You're not jabbing me with anything! You'd fuck it up!"

The truth was that I knew exactly where he kept it and that it was past its expiry date. I couldn't exactly tell him that, though. And mostly I'd use other kinds of oil so that I could piss him off without running the risk of having to call an actual ambulance to save his worthless parasitic ass. Didn't want to have to make any tough choices if he stopped breathing in front of me.

As his reactions got bigger and more profane, I refined my approach. I put a burned-out light bulb in the reading lamp near his little bed, waited for him to replace it, then switched it back. I did that four times.

I probably had too much fun and he suspected that I was messing with him, especially as the hot water kept on running out whenever he took a shower. Not always. Just a lot.

He made a subtle accusation. "You're turning the hot water off, you little shit!" I denied everything, used my best shocked-and-innocent face, and even patiently showed him how the circuit breaker for the water heater trips all the time, and the hot water just runs out. He didn't believe me and told Mom.

She shut him down - no way was her son doing anything that immature. And I had made sure the hot water had run out on her once, just as insurance. She probably knew that I was up to something. I think she used her defense of me as a way of standing up to Gary.

They had a big argument about me and his voice took on a tone. It was a tone that lit my brain up with both fear and anger and I paced my room listening intently for signs that Mom might need help and identifying household items in each room that I could hit him with. Always best to use something close to hand, I figured.

I didn't want him taking things out on Mom. I just wanted to get rid of him. I let things lie for a few days and then applied myself to bringing things to a satisfactory conclusion.

# Chapter Five

## Pranks, Poison and a Happy Dance

The answer to the question of how to get rid of the GareBear for good was his relationship to his car. It was a 2008 Pontiac Grand Prix. They don't make them anymore - oversized, overpowered, and underwhelming in all other ways, and the GareBear loved it like the child he never had. And he HATED it when I pronounced it *Grand Pricks*.

Its existence invited my attention. I half-deflated a tire and waited for him to notice. He drove away and returned with it filled. I did it again the next day. And the next. Then, when he returned from having it "repaired," I deflated a different tire. Repeatedly. Then I started my light bulb trick on his signal lights. It took some time and a couple of tools, as the good people at Pontiac seemed to be looking for extra business for mechanics when they designed the lights, but some things are worth doing.

After a couple of replacement bulbs, I found Gary in my room, looking through my stuff, not even pretending to sneak around. He found some storyboards on my desk, some of the preliminary ideas for my next project. He was ripping them in half and chucking them one by one on the floor when I entered.

"I thought you wanted to be some kinda animator. But you draw like shit, kid. These are terrible."

"You smell like shit, Gare. I'll take drawing like shit over smelling like shit any day. You should get out of my room now."

"And what are you gonna do about it if I don't?"

I just looked at him, unwilling to make a stupid threat that I couldn't follow through with.

"Tell you what," he said. "You stay away from me and my stuff, and I'll stay away from you and yours." And he held up the final storyboard sheet in his hand and violently ripped it to pieces before throwing it on the pile. He walked up to me and said in a very low voice, "It's just your pretty pictures for now, kid. Next time it might be your pretty Mommy."

That was all I needed to hear. Somehow, having him here in my own room threatening us directly removed whatever fear I might have felt. Sure, I was angry. But it was not a hit-him-over-the-head-with-a-lamp rage. It was a colder, more determined anger, one I could use.

No more pranks.

Gary had to go.

Mom's a private nurse - that's where all the shift work comes from - so she wasn't around for a lot of my efforts to rid us of the Gary menace. I could take advantage of her absence just one more time and use Gary's temper against him when I was the only one in his direct line of fire.

I set myself up to get caught in the act.

The climax would be in the kitchen, late at night. Mom was working the night shift, so I had a little more freedom of action than usual. And I was hoping that Gary Two-Step was feeling uninhibited after an evening of beer and ultimate fighting on TV. In front of me was a small mortar and pestle. To my right was a package of laxatives and I was grinding them up and sprinkling them into GareBear's box of breakfast cereal - Sugar Farts, I think, some kind of genetically modified sugar with extra gluten baked right in. I had been making noise, banging around the place in what I hoped was a furtively suspicious way, and sure enough, he pulled up in front of me in his jammies with a look of victory on his smarmy five o'clock-shadowed face.

"What do you think you're doing?" Beer breath and body odour filled the kitchen.

"Nothing."

He picked up the laxative box and looked at it. "You're poisoning me, you little shit!"

"I deny that."

"You lying bugger, I knew you were behind it."

"I am not behind anything. I don't know what you're referring to."

"If you touch my things, my clothes, my *car*, ever again, I will eliminate you, you understand?"

"No, I'm sure I don't."

"I will break your fingers off and then shove them up your ass, then I will cut you a new one and ram your snot-nosed face right up it!"

"That seems extreme."

"You just keep it up! I'm looking forward to it. And let me tell you this," he growled, his beery breath directed into my face, "as soon as I'm finished with you, I'll take care of Kelly, take care of her the way a man should take care of a woman. Think about that, kid." I was careful to remain silent, to pack the rage I felt into a perfect ball of ice and store it deep within whatever I have that might be like a soul, to be brought out and used when I needed it.

Then he did me a favour and threw the cereal and laxatives in the garbage as if that put paid to my little plan. I waited a few minutes, placed a new box of Sugar Farts in its accustomed spot, took the garbage outside and put it into one of our neighbour's bins, and checked that my phone had clearly recorded our conversation.

The next day, when Mom had come home and had some time to decompress, I played the recording for her. She looked at me sideways.

"Sure - I had his cereal box open, but I was NOT poisoning him. I was just hungry." Technically, that was true. The laxatives are not poison.

"Why did you record it?"

"He talks to me like that ... a lot." Well, one threat like that counts as a lot to me. So, again, technically not a lie.

"Did you do something to his car?"

"Nooo. The guy's paranoid." That one was a total lie, yes.

"Robinson. He means it - he's dangerous. If you've been provoking him, we're just lucky that he hasn't followed through. He's leaving. Today. Anything's better than ..." And she walked away. It made me wonder what I might have missed, what other things Gary might have done?

I didn't have much time to think about it because my brain was overcome by both those questions and an unfamiliar feeling - happiness.

The anticipation of a thing is often more satisfying than the thing itself, and I flew around the house buzzing with the joy of an ugly job nearly done. I went to where I had hidden Gary's things (an Amazon delivery box in plain view on a shelf near the back door) and I gathered them up, throwing everything into his big suitcase, making sure that he'd have neither an excuse nor an opportunity to return. I wasn't even using any of my latent rage, just the good spirit of a job well done.

Mom carefully packed up all his stuff, from his greasy dandruff comb to his sad sleeveless undershirts, and dirty socks. Alarm clock, chargers, crumpled-up receipts, everything that had a Gary vibe or stink went into a big suitcase, a small carry-on, and a couple of garbage bags.

It was a monument to our imprisonment and it grew taller, sprouting awkward limbs that threatened to send it toppling over. The physical record of his life, stacked like garage-sale leftovers, reeked of small-time failure. Now that he was on his way out, I determined to find out, to demand an answer to the question that she had always avoided. Why had Mom let him stay here? What reason could she have possibly had to let this troll ruin our home?

For now, that question would wait and my brain was transfixed, awash in happy brain chemicals in anticipation of the next scene, the one where Mom threw GareBear out. Where he took his shit and disappeared.

It was epically satisfying when it happened.

He returned from getting a tire fixed. The artifacts of his existence here greeted him by the door. He came in and saw his stuff and a look of surprise, and then anger, transformed his face.

"What's all this?"

"Your stuff. You're leaving, Gary."

"You can't kick me out! Not with what I know!"

"That's right. But I'm doing it anyway. Whatever you do, you can't stay here anymore." Then he looked at me, standing behind Mom with my finger poised above the 1 on my phone, ready to give it the second push.

"He told you, didn't he? Did he say what he was doing?"

"I heard," she said. "Poisoning you."

Wow, I thought. Nice move.

"And that's okay with you?"

"You threatening him isn't okay with me, Gary. I don't know what he was doing, but you're the dangerous one here. Nothing is worth this. Go ahead - do your worst, but if you aren't gone in two minutes, we're calling the police."

"You won't call the cops! You wouldn't dare! We have business!"

"No, Gary. We have nothing."

I don't know what he meant about business. Mom threw his stuff out onto the front step in full view of the neighbours, who were now doing what neighbours are good for - watching our little drama unfold. They got a good show. Gary was crazy mad, sputtering and swearing, his fists balled up and his face red with rage.

"You will be sorry. You and that shit of a kid!" He pointed past Mom at me and I smiled and waved back. "This is not over," he shouted over his shoulder as he loaded his stuff in his car. And he left in a silvery puff of Grand Prix. Safe and sound and definitely not dead, by the way.

A gloriously crowd-pleasing denouement. The world was a better place. I sang a happy song as I went to the hardware store, bought new locks and installed them on our doors. I almost danced through the neighbourhood, making sure that people knew that Gary was no longer welcome and that they should call the cops if they saw him.

At the end of Mom's long and stressful day, she seemed to be content. She smiled at me and I let her hug me, and I couldn't quite figure out how she was feeling. Like she knew something bad was going to happen, but that it would ultimately be better than the way things had been. As for me, I didn't know about anything bad, but I was sure things were already better. And forget that bit about the anticipation of a thing being better than the thing itself.

Gary's absence was matchless.

# Chapter Six

## We Also Have Most of Our Teeth

To fully understand the disruption that Gary had constituted you have to get Mom and me. First - I am *not* a rebellious drug-taking drop-out porn addict. Second - Mom is *not* an emotionally distant self-involved alcoholic.

She has an okay job. I have a crappy-but-okay-for-now job. We have enough to eat.

Good for us.

Because it would be understandable if we were more damaged.

Most of me you can sort of figure out by understanding my name. Knowing who I am and why I am, it kind of figures. Mom had told me the story in bits and pieces, a little more each year as I got older and better able to understand. She and Dad met and fell in love. They were really young. I came along maybe a little sooner than they expected. It was hard. Dad didn't have a job that would support us, so Mom and I had to live with her parents.

Dad didn't get along with Mom's parents and pressured her to leave. When he found a job and an apartment, he got his way. My grandparents didn't want Mom to leave, but she thought she had to, that she needed to give Dad and the whole marriage thing a chance.

Stuff happened. The kind of stuff that she couldn't tell me until I was finished with the Kids profile on Netflix. There was stress, money problems, maybe a mental health issue or two, and loud arguments. No fairy tale happy time. Apparently, there were also psycho control and anger issues leaking from one spouse and splashing everywhere. Obsessive love, as they say, is not love at all.

Dad hit Mom.

And when I learned that, he stopped being Dad and became Whatshisname.

When you're a boy, not even a little one, and you are told that your father used to hurt your mom, your feelings are confused, conflicted. Boys want to admire and identify with their dads. But hitting your mom? No way. And for some reason you feel guilty, like you did something wrong, that your existence somehow just made bad things happen. Like a little two-year-old could ever do anything to protect his mother from an abusive father.

A seventeen-year-old was different. I could do something about Gary, so I did.

Getting older, you find more complex reasons to feel guilt. Especially if you think your mother is not happy and your existence is part of the reason. I know that's not true, but feelings are feelings. And if that makes me feel protective of my mother, even if she doesn't trust me enough to be honest with me, who's gonna blame me?

So I grew up having this last name that always reminded me of something negative that I don't remember experiencing. I don't even have any reliable memories of ol' Whatshisname, just some soft-focus images of times and places he must have inhabited. I don't think Mom would have ever told me about him at all, but I was a real pain in the ass about not having a dad, and she has an honest streak, something that she has had cause to regret once in a while.

I asked Mom once why she didn't change my name. "Because I want you to be your own person. And if you think about it Chase Robinson sounds like a movie title, and that's cool."

My name, then, makes me feel weirdly guilty and creatively engaged at the same time.

Amy's name is more like the title of a novel.

Amy Stone.

She is the novel to my animated feature film; she is subtle and verbal while I am visual and people call me blunt. She likes precision and language and I prefer the broad strokes of a well-framed image. That applies to life as well as art. Not that I think we should all act without thinking, but when you know that there's a problem, you have to act. I cannot be a useless Hamlet, gnashing on his own knuckles while a ghost gets more done in one minor haunt than Hamlet does in an entire play.

"You just don't get him," Amy told me when I complained of his overwhelming worthlessness and of the wasted hours we had to spend with him in English class and writing about him for our final big essay assignment.

"Are you nuts? I would kill to have an evil uncle to slay. Especially if he was messing with my mother."

"Did you hear what you just said?"

"And you should hate this play. The only thing the women do in the story is fret about the men. Think about Ophelia - instead of dealing with life, she goes mad and floats away."

"If you killed my father, I might be just as ridiculous."

"No way - you're not going nuts, no matter what. And Hamlet screwing up, killing her dad the one time he actually tries to *do* something, is a good sign that he's useless. He needs to get rid of his evil uncle and just accept some consequences."

She didn't argue that point, which made me think it was a good one. Action and consequence. If you know what needs to be done, and don't do it, what sort of underachieving twerp are you?

# Chapter Seven

## It's Not Selfish if It Makes Her Happy

Those were good days, that GareBear-free time. Sure, Mom was not perfect, kind of like she got up every day expecting something bad to happen, but I knew things had changed and that she'd get over it. I'm a sensitive guy, and I hung out at home more than usual, tried to let her watch what she wanted on TV, and looked after whatever I could.

So, Loki got walked and fed and I cleaned up his crap. I did my best to air out the row house to get rid of the reek of its former inhabitant. I started washing my feet and I threw out the most hopeless of my socks, which was more of a relief than I would have imagined.

And I also pretended to let Mom look after me. I know that sounds self-serving. It's not. I'd rather she didn't. I am perfectly happy with my own lousy cooking when I don't mistake cayenne pepper for seasoned salt. I can do laundry, and I prefer the house cleaner than she does (and she sucks at cleaning anything), so there are no self-reliance issues around here. But I think she feels guilty about how much she has to work to pay the rent, so when she is around, I have to let the genes that control her maternal instincts express themselves.

I did more than that. I had friends over. And even better, one of them was Amy. Mothers love it when their sons have friends who are girls because they think that their parenting has had benefits, that their influence is somehow proven to be positive, indicated by the presence of a female who is not forced to be here.

Fair enough. Maybe they have a point. Don't care.

Our friendship, the one between Amy and me, has nothing to do with me. I am her friend because she is willing to be mine. She is quicker in math, smarter in English, and way better looking, although that's not actually saying much but I mean mad crazy better looking. And she is more socially gifted than I can ever be. She is just herself wherever she goes.

So, Rich, Carter, Amy and I let Mom make dinner for us, a big messy spaghetti dinner with Italian sausage and tonnes of bread and stinky cheese. She liked it, we liked it.

Mom always takes the opportunity to say personal things to my friends, which is an unending embarrassment for me. That night she picked on Rich.

"I like your hair," she said.

"Oh, thanks." Rich was also suitably embarrassed, maybe as much for me as for himself. Inevitably, Mom kept going.

"Dreadlocks?"

"I'm trying, yeah, but my grandmother was Swedish and there must be some anti-dreads genes in me somewhere. Just can't get the right vibe."

"Dreads? Oh, yeah, I get it. Cool," Carter said, mouth open, gazing at Rich like it was the first time he'd ever seen him. Carter should only be allowed to wear one t-shirt, extra-large for his bulked-up muscly-ness, one that says OBLIVIOUS.

Amy helped clean up. I helped too, making it appear to Amy that I was contributing but not so much that I took away from Mom's attempt to cleanse her guilt. Rich and Carter watched YouTube on Rich's phone.

"I'm outta here," Mom said as the last dish was washed.

"What? Where are you going?" I had expected her to hang around and eavesdrop, or at least talk to Amy.

"Just out for a bit. Won't be late." She picked a jacket up from the hooks near the door, palmed her car keys and was gone. She'd done that a few times recently, and because I didn't want her to always ask me where I was going, I didn't ask her.

So, great, I thought. I still had a bunch of the GareBeer, the beer I'd stolen one at a time from our previous house guest. So as long as we finished them fast and covered our tracks, everyone would be happy. Four tabs were pulled and the conversation changed.

I knew that Gary had phoned a few times, proving that he was still not dead. At first, it seemed as if he was trying to convince Mom of something. The last couple of calls were more foreboding. Mom wouldn't tell me anything when I asked if he was threatening her. It didn't seem to faze her much, though, and she just said that she'd taken care of things so there was nothing to be concerned about. While I wasn't worried about him, I was watching and waiting for the day when he would just go away, when we wouldn't have to think about him anymore.

One of the ways I had invented to rid my brain of all things Gary-related was to consider the future of my mother's social life.

"So, I need some ideas."

"Yes, you do. First, steal better beer. This stuff's skunky," Carter complained.

"Not my choice. And what I meant was that I need some ideas about how to prevent the occurrence of the GareBear incident."

"You mean a boyfriend moving in?" asked Rich.

"You can't control your mother's personal life," Amy said firmly.

"I know - I just want to influence it. I need her to go out with a better class of guy, someone who's good enough, preferably *too* good for her."

"Well," drawled Carter, "she *is* ..."

"Don't say it!"

"I was going to say, well disposed in the matronly mother-of-my-friend kinda way."

"Yeah, so what you need to do is make a plan," Rich added.

"No you don't. It's none of your business." Amy wasn't getting it. Mom couldn't be trusted. I had to be pre-emptive.

"Of course it's my business. If the G-Bear hadn't got kicked out, I might be dead. You shoulda heard him threaten me."

"You provoked him," Amy objected.

"And you told me to get creative. It was a sooner-or-later kind of choice for me. A guy who says things like that is going to find his reasons. So, it was him or me, and I'm too attached to me to even consider the other option."

"What exactly do you think you can do to influence the quality of your mom's boyfriends?" Carter was a complete skeptic about my ability to do anything.

"I'll show you," I replied, leading everyone over to the kitchen table to where I had our family laptop. "Mom uses one online dating site in particular. Her profile depends on her stated preferences as indicated by the site's questionnaire. I know all her passwords, because she trusts me way too much, and I can change her profile to attract a more desirable sort of person."

"This is a bad idea," Amy said.

"What do you need us for?" asked Rich.

"I need help redoing the profile so that their computer will match her with a better class of men."

"Good-byeeee!" sang Amy as she picked up her jacket and headed for the door.

"Wait - I'm relying on you especially. You'll know the best answers!"

"No way. Forget it. It's not a good idea. Don't do it. There. Those are the only answers I have. See ya!" The door did not hit her on the way out, but just about.

"Crap. There just went my best chance to fix this."

"Dude, we're still here," Carter said after taking a very big swig of the beer he didn't like. "We're smart. We can help you massage this."

"Yeah, no problem," said Rich. "And what's the worst thing that can happen? You already had the actual worst and his name was Gary."

He had a good point.

So, we dove in. Most of the profile we had to leave the way it was because the changes would have been too obvious, but we altered a few things hoping Mom wouldn't notice. Upped the age range a bit, to get older losers rather than younger ones, hoping they'd at least be more financially stable. We changed it so that Mom looked a little more physically active than she really is, hoping to keep out sloths like GareBear. Made sure to tick the box indicating she was not looking for someone who had kids. I know, sounds hypocritical, but I didn't need to be an instant babysitter for some boyfriend's kid. We figured that a small-business owner would be nice, so we emphasized the importance of occupation. And I changed the box that said Divorced to Widowed. I figured that was less complicated and more truthful because we had no actual evidence that my father was alive.

Why that mattered to me, I don't know.

We finished, covered our tracks and that was that. I don't think Mom looked at it for quite a while, as she was understandably off men for a bit, but it felt like I'd accomplished something, made progress toward the desired state.

And the universe took one step forward and two steps back.

# Chapter Eight

## She Means Lazy and Useless in the NICE Way

There were cops in my living room. That's not normally a good sign. A man and a woman, from their voices, and both sounded really seriously suspicious. Of Mom.

The day had already been suspicious. A documentary in History, a movie in English, soccer in Phys Ed, and a substitute in Math. No headaches, no homework, no worries. Suspicious.

But I came from school to the rented row house we called home and I saw the car outside. It wasn't a patrol car, but no cop is hard to spot, with telltale cheap wheel coverings and a totally officious vibe. I paused briefly and decided that there was no need to panic, to run, or alternately to concoct an alibi. I had every right to breeze in the back way, take station in the kitchen, and eavesdrop on the conversation. I was lucky to get there near the beginning. I could hear all three voices clearly - Mom, and two police detectives, who I thought of as ManCop and CopWoman. I know, it's immature, but I cannot be intimidated by people who have stupid names, even if I'm the one inventing them.

"... investigating an incident involving him yesterday." If the cops were asking questions about a "him," it had to be about the GareBear. Maybe he was accused of public indecency or impersonating a human being.

"Okay." Mom's tone of voice was wary.

"He stayed here for a period of several months did he not?" That was ManCop. They alternated questions, back and forth, as if it was a way to keep Mom off-balance. Or maybe that gave them time to write her answers down.

"Yes."

"And he left, or perhaps was thrown out a couple of weeks ago?"

"That's right."

"Have you had any contact with him since that time?" ManCop delivered the question with that special, "We can find out if you're lying" tone that police have.

"He phoned me. Mostly to shout at me." That was for sure. I'd heard the tinny shouts from the speaker all the way in the other room.

"Would I be correct in assuming that you were not on good terms with him when he left?"

"I kicked him out. He was lazy and useless and he threatened my son."

"So your son and Mr. Twolan - they didn't get along?"

"What do you think?"

"Do you know where he was staying after you ... threw him out?" ManCop's tone was even more skeptical now, as if he really wanted to say that Mom had done something much more sinister.

"With someone ... a Cherie, Cheryl, something like that."

"Ms. Cheryl McCallum," said CopWoman. "She called for help, but it was too late."

Too late?

"You know, it's interesting that you haven't asked us what happened," CopWoman commented.

"Okay, so what happened?"

"Seems like it was some kind of anaphylaxis. Allergic to ... something." ManCop apparently didn't want to give anything away.

"Gary is ... was allergic to nuts. What does any of this have to do with me?"

"This is just routine. Nothing to worry about." CopWoman had a phony casual tone that contradicted her words. "Thank you for your cooperation. We'll be in touch." When I heard that I sped to the back stairs and ever-so-carefully eased the door closed so that they didn't see me on the way out.

And they left.

We all die but remarkably few of us are murdered, especially when you consider how many of us are total shits. I wondered what the police thought was the case with Gary. If they knew what a complete asshole he was, they were going to suspect someone did him in for the greater good. Maybe that's why they were here.

"How was school?" she asked, looking into the street as the cops pulled away. I had emerged from my hidey-hole.

"You know. The same."

"I have some ... bad ... news."

"I know. I heard. And, I dunno about bad."

"Are you okay?"

"Me? Of course - are YOU?"

"Yeah." She stared into the middle distance, thinking about ... something.

"You know what's weird - he had an EpiPen."

"Maybe no one was there to use it."

"Mom - they sounded suspicious."

"Hmm? I suppose they did. Cops are always suspicious."

"I guess they're supposed to be."

"If you were listening you know that I didn't tell them."

"Tell them what?"

"That he accused you of trying to poison him."

"Oh yeah. That. That's good because I did NOT try to poison him, you know."

"You ... you deleted that recording, right Robinson?"

"For sure. *Kelly.*"

"Just as well."

She gave me a hug then. Mom's a big hugger, so that's nothing unusual. But when I thought about it, other things were. Why ask me about the recording? She didn't suspect ME, did she? Where was her unconditional motherly faith? And why was she not more upset? The police would be curious about that. I know she kicked him out, but she'd let him move in to begin with, so she had to have liked him at some point, at least a little. She should have at least pretended to care.

---

For a couple of hours after the cops left, she was mostly just thoughtful, quiet, maybe a little nervous. She looked out the window a lot as if expecting someone to pull up. And she kept sneaking looks at me. I know, because I kept sneaking looks at her.

It was kind of quiet around the ol' row house that evening. I sat texting my friends with the news. Mom sat staring into her computer screen, brow furrowed, giving her nails a good chew. That made me nervous, hoping that she wouldn't discover that I'd tampered with her dating profile. That couldn't be what she was looking at, I mean it would be weird if we got news about one old boyfriend dying, maybe even getting murdered, and she's looking for another relationship.

Okay, okay, she was probably just looking up recipes.

She never looks up recipes.

And she had a hard expression on her face. Maybe it was a good thing. Maybe she was forming calluses over her feelings, like regular women in their forties do. You know - calluses that result when a husband or partner works all day and golfs all weekend. Calluses that help you survive when your teenage daughter is a self-involved narcissist and hates you. Calluses caused by your lying, nerdy teenage son.

Or ... the kind of callus that develops when someone dies, and you're okay with it.

# Chapter Nine

## It's Not Paranoia if It's True

"What sort of paranoid *are* you?"

Amy was not impressed.

We sat on a bus stop bench and watched six lanes of traffic zip past. Amy was dressed all in denim for the cool day, covered up but for a strip of ankle showing up between her shoes and her jeans. Her long light-coloured hair fell loosely to her shoulders and as I looked at her I wondered for the zillionth time, why does this girl hang out with me?

"I am not paranoid. It's simple deduction. If you're allergic to peanuts, then they're poison. Poison is predominantly used by women when they choose to murder someone. It's not a guy thing."

"Who said that he has been murdered? Who said anything about poison?"

"No one, yet, but it was clear if you read between the lines. And Mom herself mentioned the poison."

"You're the one who tried to poison him."

"That was a ruse! I was just provoking him."

"Why would your mother murder the guy? He was gone."

"Gone, yes. No longer a threat? I dunno. I still don't know why she put up with him for such a long time."

"Meaning that you're engaging your overactive imagination."

"You can't blame me for thinking about things. And you weren't there. Mom said that I should back off and let her do what she had to do, that she'd take care of him. I didn't realize it at the time, but she could have been talking about getting rid of Gary permanently."

"You should have thought things through before you provoked him. Dad says that he was bad news."

My mind was spinning or I might have asked why her dad had an opinion about Gary Two-Step when he hadn't even met the guy. And I couldn't help but think that if Mom had set it all up, found some way to kill Gary from a distance, the world without Gary was better than the world with him. And really, it was in self-defence. Even though I didn't know what he was threatening her with, the threats were real.

We left the bench and headed up the street to the Heights, well known around town as the most depressingly empty mall that had not yet been torn down for condos or box stores. My shift at the grocery store started at two. Eight hours of shifting boxes and stocking shelves. It would give me a lot of time to think.

Amy was headed for the transitway. She planned to get to the new and only slightly clunky light rail system. The trains ran, but some things in some stations still functioned only sometimes - things like security cameras and washrooms. Don't get mugged or have to pee were the rules. She was going downtown. Probably to meet BOB.

BOB who-was-studying-software-engineering BOB.

I always said his name like that.

BOB, with an overly long O and really bouncing Bs. Amy hated it. I didn't care, because I was not fond of BOB. Why would I be - he was older and better looking than me and he was dating Amy. It was not possible for me to like him. I don't think he liked me either, although I can't imagine why he would have been threatened by my scrawny presence in Amy's life.

I didn't ask what she was up to. I didn't want to think about her doing something with BOB, laughing and enjoying herself when I wasn't there, looking at him with the same eyes she smiled at me with, putting her hand on his forearm or her head on his shoulder like she never did with me. In my head, I wrote my own version of her afternoon, made her go shopping for girl stuff. Not that I have any idea what that is.

Amy and I had been friends since Grade 6. We were in the same class and had to do a project together, something about human rights and women and war. Over the course of the last five years, we've often been in the same class, gone to the same party, had the same friends. I guess it hadn't occurred to her that she'd matured and become gorgeous and I had matured and become … taller. She was fit and smooth-skinned and perfect, and I was just me, occasionally zit-faced, and plain. She shouldn't be hanging out with me.

Amy didn't have a family any bigger than mine. She had an uncle who died a long time ago, but that was about it except for some faraway grandparents. Her divorced parents had interesting jobs - her mom, Marissa Iraklidis, was actually a theatre director or producer or something and her dad, Jason Stone, had a corner office and a punchy title with Crown in the name. When I saw her dad, he mostly just grinned and said Hi, like Amy and I were still twelve and playing on a mixed softball team together. I suppose the worst thing about him was that he loved his job. Amy mostly lived with him because her mother travelled for months at a time. He wasn't around a lot, either, but he did come home at night.

Her mom, though, always gave me the broadest smile which was friendly but at the same time disappointed, a smile that said it was fine that I was taking up limited Amy-time, but that she should probably think about doing better. Amy called her mom a drama queen in both a literal and figurative sense. Her ability to make all of life's small foibles into intimately personal dramas drove Amy's dad away, she thought.

My mother is not dramatic in the least. She's about as matter-of-fact as the ripping-off of a band-aid. *Some things just hurt* is her motto.

So, Amy got to travel, you know Tuesday in Los Angeles with Mom and Friday in Toronto with Dad, and go to parties with artsy people who wore black and had fashion eyewear instead of glasses. It all added up to a life in which there should have been little to no room for someone like me. Especially when BOB was part of the equation. I didn't tell her that, though. I'm not stupid. I wanted the ride to last for as long as possible.

It was later, about five o'clock, when Rich showed up at work and found me in the breakfast cereal aisle building a wall of yellow boxes with smiling cartoon bears on them. I was supposed to stack them right up onto the fourth shelf. I guess little old ladies didn't buy this stuff because they'd never be able to reach it. I was stretching upwards when he tapped me on the shoulder. It startled me and I dropped the box. Hope someone likes crushed Crap-ee-os.

"Did you hear?"

"Did I hear you approach me from behind? No." I picked up the box and looked past Rich to make sure there were no lurking managers.

"I know that - did you hear the news?"

"Will you just tell me?"

"Your former stay-at-home slimeball - I thought you should know. It's on Twitter. The media are reporting a source saying that his death was suspicious. The cops are refusing to comment, but you know what that means, right? It's kinda cool. I've never known anyone who was murdered before."

I must have made a dopey face because Rich gave me a nudge.

"Hey, are you alright?"

"Hmm? Yeah, sure. Fine." I had to stop myself from phoning home and making sure Mom was there and not in custody.

"What are you doing tomorrow?"

"Nothing, yet."

"Wanna play FIFA 20? Maybe get some pizza?"

"Sure, sure," I said.

We left it at that and Rich wandered off. I still had half a shift to go. I finished with the cereal aisle and carried the empty boxes into the back. I pulled out my phone and texted Mom.

**Me**: You there?

**Mom**: Aren't you working?

**Me**: On a break. Heard about it?

**Mom**: The so-called story? Yup.

**Me**: Still think I did it?

**Mom**: Never did.

And that was that. She didn't bother to tell me it wasn't her.

I went back to work feeling a little relieved but with a nagging, unsettled feeling. I wondered if the police were suspicious of the woman whose house he'd been living in. Was it possible that they thought she'd killed him after experiencing only a couple of weeks of his charms? She'd make me look like a serious underachiever. Like Hamlet.

Then again, maybe she was the source of the story. Maybe she figured the death was as suspicious as I did.

I told myself that was why I was feeling uneasy, that I was feeling guilty that I wasn't more upset that Gary was dead. My conscience told me that I should be more shocked, more saddened by the passing of someone I knew.

Considering that I was responsible.

Not at fault. Just responsible.

# Chapter Ten
## I. Am. So. Stupid.

This was The Plan.

Like most people my age, I am a mixed bag of potential, some of it even good. And, while I have the potential to be creative and productive, I require focus and organization to make sure I don't succumb to my reality deficit, my hard-wired preference for dreaming long term. Short-term stuff, the actual work that goes into getting anywhere in the future, that's what I suck at.

My manager at work, who always needs everything done, like, five minutes ago, is a short-term kind of person. And I spend most of my working hours trying to avoid him. At home, I need an omnipresent, live-in means of reducing my reality gap. A few threats, maybe an ultimatum or two. The occasional match lit under my butt. That's all I need. From Mom. As long as she doesn't get sent up for killing Gary.

The Plan first calls for short-term dues-paying. I work. I save money. I get into a college animation program. I will learn, impressing everyone with my adroit, edgy creativity. My self-deprecating good humour and fresh, insightfully comedic take on themes both classic and contemporary will take over. And I can totally do all the team-player bullshit, too. That'll be me, the worker bee.

Elbowing out competition from lesser drones, next I will slide into an entry-level job at a local studio. Anyone with a brain will see the potential that I can make them millions while expressing my uncompromised artistic vision.

There I go long-terming again. My reality gap, stretching away to infinity.

On the road from now until then, I need a couple of things. First, I have to learn how to actually draw, not just think about drawing. I can kind of do stick people now, so I don't have as far to go as I used to. I'll get there. That's why I wasn't too upset when Gary destroyed my storyboards. Stick people don't take too long.

I'm composing or recomposing a storyboard for my animated feature - regular guy gets unhinged and becomes a vigilante, but with no tights, mask, or alter ego. He exacts revenge or retribution on, maybe even justice from, the predatory creatures who typically ruin the urban landscape. And subvocalizes in a deep raspy voice.

Wait - maybe some of them are parasites, not predators.

Doesn't matter. I'm all over it. As soon as I can figure out what form revenge or maybe justice would be served, I will have a story. And he has to do it without superpowers. And it has to be funny.

There were a few things distracting me from my project though, not the least of which was the continuing presence of jerky men in Mom's life. They crawl out from under slime-encrusted rocks, plug into the internet and scout for easy prey. They're the type who ooze masculine charm, who project well-adjusted sensitive-new-age-man confidence when they find that someone's online dating status is "widow."

Holy shit, that was stupid.

There was Mom bathed in the glow of her laptop - typing, scrolling, clicking, and furrowing her brow. She was looking at emails from and profiles of men. I know, because I know all her passwords. And her problem was surfacing again. It seems to be a local sport for forty or fifty-ish creeps to get online and chase widows. And this time it was even more my fault. I had done it.

I had been the widow maker.

And when the dust settled, there was Don. Big Don Buckley.

My scheme had worked perfectly. Horribly perfectly. We had changed the fancy date-o-matic thingamabobber to attract a different sort of loser. Yes, the operative word is loser. I think that Carter, Rich and I had managed to find someone that we might have wanted to date if we wanted to date older men. That's what Amy said when I showed her his online profile.

Of course, she was right. We seemed to be into good-looking athletic types who were in business for themselves. He, Big Don, was very fond of his own rugged good looks, judging by the number of photos he posted. A lot of them were taken at the university athletics centre where Don said he was a kinesiology "Associate."

Once I discovered the correspondences between Don and Mom had translated into coffee dates, a sure precursor to him moving in and ruining my life, I decided action was required. She'd kill me if she ever found out, but I felt that my vested interest in my own well-being was justification for a little proactive snooping.

I went to the gym and asked for him. Turns out he was an underemployed personal trainer, he played professional football for all of nine games over two seasons and what he wanted was for a woman to send him to massage therapy school so that he could get a job on a cruise ship. I found that out by talking to the woman at the desk.

"Oh, you want Big Don? I haven't seen him much lately. You related?"

"No. Why do you ask?"

"You don't look like one of his clients."

"They're older and likely to be more female than me, right?"

"You said it."

It's pretty much my only superpower. I'm totally harmless. People look at me and see an awkward teenage guy with crooked teeth and bad hair and they tell me anything. And I've learned how to ask questions.

"So, is Don busy a lot? I think I may have a client for him."

"Busy? I doubt it. I can't say why, but I'd be surprised."

"Just between you and me, I'm looking to buy my mother some personal training time for her birthday and, not having a lot of money to throw around, I'm checking a few people out. Is Don ... the trustworthy hard-working type?" I smiled my best conspiratorial smile, the one that says, "Please help me out. I need just the right sort of good person, like you, right now."

"Don't waste your time," she said quietly. "The first chance he gets, he's taking a job on a cruise ship as a masseur. He just needs some cash up front to take a course and for travel. But you never heard this from me."

"Gotcha. Thanks," I said warmly.

So Big Don wants the world to think he's a professor but he just wants to go knead septuagenarian buttocks on the Lido deck. Didn't sound too bad. We don't have any money he could scam. Mom's car was worthless. The only thing we had was a good credit rating.

And some savings for my college animation tuition.

Shit!

I got home as fast as I could, which took awhile on the bus. I spent some of the time texting Amy.

**Me**: You were right.
**Amy**: I'm always right.
**Me**: Big Don Buckley.
**Amy**: Scuse me?
**Me**: The guy that our new dating profile chose for Mom.
**Amy**: What about him?
**Me**: Just checked him out where he works.
**Amy**: Oh, that's gonna turn out well.
**Me**: A disaster.
**Amy**: Yes, you are.

I hit the ground running after I got off the bus and sprinted homeward. I still had no plan, no idea how I was going to deal with Big Don. How do I tell Mom how I know that he's on the make for a sucker? She'd take it personally that I think she needs protecting, let alone that I'm spying on her.

As I rounded the final corner on the way home, I spotted a strange truck parked in front of our place. It was an old off-roader, the kind with knobby tires so big that you have to climb into it. Just the sort of thing Big Don would tool around in. He had to be inside.

I stopped short. What do I say if I go in? Am I a good enough actor to pretend I don't know all about him? Should I start deflating his tires now, or wait for him to move in?

I decided to wait it out. Mom had an overnight shift tonight and would have to get ready. If it really was Big Don, he'd have to leave fairly soon. He doesn't know what I look like, I figured, so there's no need to hide. Just wait and watch.

I stood there, tormenting myself by imagining increasingly cringy scenarios. Maybe he was just swindling Mom out of her last dime so that he would get to go off and tickle the pressure points of appreciative old ladies on a Stars of the Shopping Channel Celebrity Cruise.

"Your fingers are magic, Donny!"

"Not as magical as your bank account, Delores."

It got worse as I began to wonder what he was doing in our house. What *they* were doing in there.

Again, shit.

The front door opened. Of course, I recognized him from his many self-reverential pictures online. He practically danced down the stairs in his too-young haircut, form-fitting t-shirt and luminescent runners. The entire *him* of him made me want to beat my head bloody against the sidewalk.

This. Is. All. My. Fault.

He started up his old truck and took off, leaving me in a cloud of blue exhaust. I gave Mom another minute and walked in.

"What were you doing just standing out there?" she asked as soon as she saw me. As always, I came up with a quick answer.

"I dunno."

When I say that, she knows she's not going to be able to get anything satisfying out of me, so she just let it go, maybe supposing that I was just in some weird teenager headspace. I eliminated all possibility of further questioning anyway. I had a question of my own, if only to cover myself.

"Who was that?"

She looked at me blankly, as if she didn't know who I was referring to.

"The guy who left in the monster truck - Mr. Sporting Life."

"Don't start, Robinson."

"Well, you knew who I meant, Kelly."

"His name is Don and we've gone out for coffee a couple of times."

I gave her a world-weary stare, or at least the closest thing my seventeen-year-old face could manage.

"Don't worry - he's no Gary."

"That's not saying much, because Gary's not even Gary anymore." Before she could object to my callousness, I kept going. "He's not moving in, right? He's not asking for money, right?"

"No, he's not moving in."

"And the money?" I imagined for a moment that Big Don was a lot more energetic than he's been given credit for if he'd made a pitch for money already.

"He doesn't want me to give him money. But he is looking for investors."

"Investors? What does he want you to invest in?"

"Him, I guess. It's all about cash flow. He's got a small business and hopes some extra training will have a direct and immediate effect on his revenue. He's willing to give me twenty percent in sixty days. I could use the extra money."

Now, this was an interesting scam. I was sure it would be all about cash flowing from us to him. Investment is so much better than a loan. A loan you have to repay. Investment means risk. And I bet his small business never ends up making its projected revenue, so all of his investors were going to have to learn how to write off losses on their taxes. These were the points that I brought up immediately and probably too forcefully.

So I had to do a lot of backpedaling. No, I didn't think she was stupid. Yes, I knew that she was grown up and, yes, I understood that she was the one to look after our family's finances and she'd done a damn good job and I should mind my own damn business.

I didn't dare mention what I knew about his cruise ship dream or phony association with the university or anything else. I should have kept my mouth shut other than to ask WHY she needed extra money. And I didn't bother remarking on his gas-guzzling harbinger of a mid-life crisis off-road vehicle that I'm sure had never left the pavement.

I retreated, apologizing, but with the taste of victory in my mouth anyway. I had made my point, sounded my alarm, raised my flag, and that was sure to be enough to avoid any unfortunate entanglements with Big Don.

And maybe I'd just saved Mom from another loser, I told myself.

I did see Big Don again. Twice. Once when he took Mom out to dinner. I retreated to my teen cave, refusing to meet him by action if not word. Mom came home later, and I left her alone to decompress, or stretch, or core strengthen, or whatever you have to do after a date with a personal trainer. We exchanged no words the next day either, both pretending that there had been no dinner out.

The last time was a week later. I saw just a glimpse of his back as he marched to his crap truck, got in, slammed the door and took off. He had just been in the kitchen with Mom. I hadn't heard their conversation, but everything sounded friendly. I began to experience that pointy gut-level fear that you get when your luck quickly changes for the worse. And right next to that was my frozen ball of rage.

I could only imagine what she was thinking. Was she going to risk her, *our* money with Big Don? Did she think she had to help him to keep his interest? Did she really believe she couldn't do SO much better than that guy?

Did she think there was something wrong with her?

And that last question got me the most, of course, because this time it was not her fault, her bad judgement, this time it was mine. So, if anyone's thoughts turned to killing, it had to be my fault, too, right?

# Chapter Eleven

## Predators Who Take Their Time Are Parasites

"So, I guess you're not going to mow down your urban predators and parasites with superior firepower?" Amy was looking at my work-in-progress, the scratchings that would someday become a storyboard.

"Nope. One-liners, maybe."

"What else - how does an alienated vigilante shut down the urban dreck without broad-stroke senseless violence or a superpower?"

"That is the question, yes. One that my subconscious is working on. I have to give it a chance, do something mindless like stocking shelves or homework."

"Or talking to yourself."

"Yup. And there is also the issue of stakes."

"Stakes for who?"

"Everyone. Why do the parasites and predators do what they do? What happens to them if they don't? What happens if Urban Vigilante Dude cannot rein them in, can't end the hegemony of mindful thoughtlessness, can't pave over the abyss of self-involved apathy?"

"Eww. Pave? Can't he, and I think it should be *she*, plant a garden or build a rainbow over it?"

"No rainbows, except in the inclusive sense. And a garden only if they don't plant kale."

I ignored her comment about having a female protagonist. There was no way I could write for a woman, and it is not in my DNA to admit it. We were sitting on our living room couch, feet up on the old coffee table, Loki the mutt between us, exposing his belly for anyone to scratch. I was basking in the continuing glow of the return of my psychological space, revelling in the freedom to exercise creative muscles with Amy. She always asks good questions, even if my first reaction is always to be mildly pissed off.

Kelly-based issues had filled my brain for months. The GareBear issue. The date-o-matic issue. The Big Don issue. I guess they're all more or less the same thing, but it still seemed a very big pile of plans, schemes, guile, stealth, and deception, and that takes a lot of mental energy. I was just now returning to my real Plan, my Life Plan, the one where I plot my own happiness and success.

Other than the threat or risk or shadow of Big Don, things were going okay.

Mom worked a lot and left me alone to take care of the row house chores, one of which was to pick up things we needed. You know, head to the coffee shop, the pharmacy, the bakery, the produce store. All of the small trips, the tiny interactions which facilitated observation of PPs, predators and parasites, in their natural urban environment.

And it was fantastic. They were everywhere.

Commuter parasites who won't move when you need to get out of a crowded bus, parking lot parasites who are so useless that they take up two spaces, suburban garden parasites who rake their yard waste into the street, and pet-owning parasites who will pick up their dog's crap in a plastic bag but then just throw it on someone else's driveway. Millennial parasites with dead-eyed me-first attitudes about everything. I'm here, world, the parasites mutely proclaim. It's up to *you* to deal with *me*.

And the predatory types? Too easy. SUV drivers who blow past crossing guards. The minivan moms who brake for parked cars but accelerate past pedestrians. Silent killers wrapped in shimmering stretchiness and mounted on pricey bicycles who come within a hair of killing everyone in their way. Delivery drivers locked into their cellphone GPS as they weave and juke through the streets.

"And what are you, or he, alienated from?" Amy asked, bringing me back from my faraway place.

"What? Oh, everything. All-around global alienation from twenty-first-century western norms."

"You know that's not exactly everything, right?"

"Yeah, well, it'll be enough alienation so that I don't have to spread it too thin."

"You have to know what you're alienated from really well in order to be truly alienated. It's not enough just to be cranky." She gathered her hair behind her head in that completely unselfconscious way of hers and draped it over her right shoulder. And all I could think about was her hair and that I could smell her shampoo and I wished I were Loki right now getting my belly scratched.

"Maybe he's alienated from contemporary consumerism and its materialistic mind-tendrils." I thought that wasn't bad for being distracted.

"Too easy," she said.

"Alright. Challenge accepted. Dude is alienated from ... himself. He *is* a parasite. He *is* a predator. And he hates himself for it, but is only able to see these things in other people, recognizing in them all of the things he subconsciously loathes about himself."

"Now you're headed somewhere." She scrolled through a bunch of messages on her phone. "I gotta go," she said, rising from the couch and reaching for her jacket, "but it seems to me that now you get to the stakes. And make it funny. Figure that out and your indie film idea is underway."

"Oh, yeah," I replied, like bringing that together would be just another evening's casual diversion. "No problemo. See you in ComTech."

"Umm, no actually, I'm going to New York with Mom. She's all wild about doing New York-y things with me. Galleries and shopping, probably. Maybe get a new hat."

"You're gone until ...?"

"Thursday - missing four days of school, so take good notes for me." She gave my shoulder a squeeze and I wanted to hug her but held back, always aware of Chase's first Relationship Rule - be one full step behind anyone you might feel like touching, squeezing, or hugging. In this case, that meant hug back, but do not initiate hugging action.

I watched her go, missing her already, knowing that the only class we shared would be a lot more tedious, even if it was my thing - ComTech is all about photography, animation, and video production. And the comment about taking notes was a joke because our teacher posted everything online.

Not having Amy around would be dull but okay. I would miss the feeling in the pit of my gut-brain whenever I thought about meeting her but The Plan was back on track. There would be no more diversions, intrusions, deletions, or digressions.

# Chapter Twelve

## They Don't Beat People with Phone Books Anymore, Either


$B$eing fingerprinted, they tell me, doesn't take as long as it used to.

And it wasn't as messy as I thought.

Turns out, they scanned my fingerprints and then put them on file so that they could instantly deliver them to whatever analytical program they wanted. Maybe send them to the CIA, the KGB, MI5 I hoped. And just a few minutes later, there would be results, comparisons, questions. It was a pilot project and they wanted me to participate, so that makes me special.

By "they" I do mean the cops.

It was a small room with overly bright lighting, painted cindercrete block walls and stale air. How many lies have been told in this room, I wondered. Maybe this was the room I'd seen on TV, the one where the clever cop got the perv serial killer to confess simply by explaining how he was going to inform the guy's wife of everything they already knew.

Wasn't about to work with me.

I knew that I had a right to a parent or a lawyer or both to be there, but I didn't see the point, so it was just me and Detective Sergeant Reynolds. He wasn't one of those intimidating cop-types. He was no taller than me, wearing non-descript civilian clothes and had a moustache that he liked to bite between questions. I looked around for a video camera and saw one where the wall meets the ceiling. A fly crawled across the lens and I must have looked weirdly distracted as the sergeant tried to get my attention.

**Reynolds**: What do you think this is about?

**Me**: I have no idea. I was hoping you'd tell me.

**Reynolds**: Can you tell me why your fingerprints are all over everything?

**Me**: Because I leave them on things that I touch?

**Reynolds**: You know what I mean.

**Me**: No, I really don't.

If I'm sounding dead cold, or unwisely smart-assed here, neither is true. I was in a bit of a daze. A little overwhelmed by my surroundings.

**Reynolds**: On all of Gary Twolan's personal articles. All of his things, his wallet, his hairbrush, his car, even a box of condoms have your fingerprints on them.

**Me**: Oooooooh. Right. Well, I was in his car, I used to move his wallet around, and the condoms, well, I just thought it would be funny if I sort of took them. But I always put everything back, so it wasn't really stealing.

**Reynolds**: How about his eye drops? Ever take them?

Did I forget about the eye drops? Do I assume that I had and just say yes? It could be argued that since I had messed with, like, everything, my fingerprints should be on everything. But do I tell him that?

**Me**: I don't remember specifically, so I'm going to say, no.

**Reynolds**: I want you to think about it carefully.

**Me**: No.

**Reynolds**: No, you didn't touch them or no, you don't remember?

**Me**: Yes.

Detective Sergeant Reynolds got annoyed with me then. He looked at me like my history teacher had when I told him that the capital of Rome was Greece. Which, if you think about it, it kind of was.

I had given my answer, though, and I wasn't going to change it.

---

**Reynolds**: Which is it?

**Me**: Like I said - I don't remember, so I'm saying, no. I didn't touch them.

**Reynolds**: So, why would you steal things just to return them later?

**Me**: Because I was trying to get under his skin.

**Reynolds**: Why was that?

**Me**: He was a douchebag.

**Reynolds**: Ever try to poison him?

**Me**: What?

**Reynolds**: According to the woman he was living with, he accused you of trying to poison him.

**Me**: Seriously? No way, I did NOT try to poison him.

**Reynolds**: Then why do you think he said that?

**Me**: Because he was as smart as he was popular?

**Reynolds**: Maybe you were trying to do more than get under his skin?

**Me**: I was annoying him because I wanted to get rid of him.

**Reynolds**: Permanently?

**Me**: I never wanted to see him again.

**Reynolds**: I guess you got your wish. We didn't see you at his funeral.

**Me**: He had a funeral?

**Reynolds**: That surprises you?

**Me**: In a way. Nobody liked him.

**Reynolds**: Some people less than others, evidently.

**Me**: Is there anything else you'd like to know?


Then he just stared at me. In the eye. For an uncomfortably long period of time, as if they taught him how to do this on one long afternoon at interrogation school. The lingering-eye-contact method of extracting a confession. I stared back at him, well-practiced in this game. If you can win a staring contest with a dog, you can beat any mere human.

That's when they let me go. I knew there was nothing else. They didn't have anything else. I had to wait though, before heading home. It turns out that when the cops take you in for questioning, they don't have to take you home.

And my only potential ride was being questioned herself.

# Chapter Thirteen

## We All Need a Little Reasonable Doubt

"**W**hat were you doing talking to them by yourself?" There was more than a note of reprimand in her voice. There was alarm.

"I knew they weren't going to bring you in with me - they were questioning you, too, right?"

The cops had taken us in separately. You know, in case we were conspiring to cover up the GareBear's murder. As if we wouldn't have already had time to get our stories straight.

"You should have had a lawyer!"

"Do we qualify for legal aid?"

"I doubt it - almost no one does."

"Then, you're welcome. We can keep our money."

"But police can trick you, get you to say things you don't even mean!"

"Well, I have a good defence. I didn't do anything wrong. Did they make a point of asking you about eye drops?"

"Did they ask *you*?"

"They said my fingerprints were all over everything and then asked me whether or not I touched his eye drops."

Mom furrowed her brow.

"Why would they say that your fingerprints are all over everything?"

"Because they are."

"And ...?"

"And I used to mess with GareBear's head a little. Take things, then put them back. Just to annoy him."

"So maybe your prints *were* on the eye drops."

"Why would they ask me about the eye drops if my prints were on them. If they found my fingerprints on them, then I logically must have touched them. So why ask?"

"They asked me about them, too."

"Same question, then - if your fingerprints were on them, why ask you?"

"Maybe nobody's prints were on them - except Gary's."

"But why did they care?" I looked at her real hard, showing that I expected her to be able to give me an answer.

"No idea."

And that was that. No further outrage, no high-pitched diatribe about the injustice of subjecting her son to an interrogation room and a guy with a bad moustache.

She seemed to have recovered quickly. Mom was not worried about me.

That got me going. If she was not worried it meant that she was sure I hadn't done anything more than charmingly mischievous. That's not right. Even if she believes me, she's supposed to be worried. She needed to show everyone, demonstrate her maternal instincts so that people wouldn't get suspicious. Everyone, especially the cops, likes to judge people on the basis of how they should react in a given situation. That we all tend to react differently from each other, in seriously unpredictable ways, doesn't seem to matter.

If all of this was bothering me, how was the Great Detective getting any sleep at all? How could his moustache stand up to all the gnashing it was going to get? You know, missing fingerprints, a victim loathed by way more than half the population, all the means, motive, and opportunity stuff.

I wondered what he might be pondering as he tossed and turned in bed beside the wife at night. Means and opportunity. Mom had them both. She understood the effects of peanut oil when applied to the eyeball of someone like Gary. Allergic, I mean, not just a douchebag. From the detective's point of view, she could have planted it on him when she packed up his things to throw him out.

Motive was probably puzzling him, though. I probably had the means and the opportunity as well, but not much of a motive. But Detective Sergeant Reynolds might be looking at me anyway, given that I'm the more likely perpetrator if you ignore the whole poisoning thing. Men murder way more than women. If anyone really hated Gary it was me, but Reynolds may not have known that.

I could see how it might all happen. If you wanted Gary dead all you had to do was to get him to expose *himself* to nuts. What better way than a little peanut oil in the eye drops? I could picture how it was done. Just use his customary eye drops to suck up some peanut oil from any garden-variety natural peanut butter. Next time he gets itchy eyes it's curtains. You get him to kill himself at a distance and time of his choosing. I wondered if the cops knew his EpiPen had expired. I wondered if they knew that *I* knew.

When I went over it with Amy she was more than skeptical. We were sitting at the coffee shop, about halfway between her place and mine. Back from New York, she told me about museums and galleries (turns out that they're different, which was serious news to me) and Fifth Avenue, the Village and the High Line. I told her about my quality time with the police and my eye drops hypothesis.

"Did the police actually say he was killed by peanut oil in the drops?"

"No, but they were specifically curious about them. And I know that my fingerprints should have been there. I have a clear memory of the bottle. If there were no prints, they were wiped."

"By your own mother? You're delusional!"

"I'm completely rational. She didn't know she was wiping mine, just hers."

"Maybe someone else tampered with the drops and wiped the bottle."

"Who else wants him dead?"

"Exactly - why do you think your mother wanted him dead any more than any other woman he's ever met?" To be fair, Gary was a greater threat to womankind than to mankind. For the cops, though, it only argued that Mom was more likely to have killed him than I was. "Besides, just because you're relieved that he's gone doesn't mean that either you or your mom murdered him."

I had to admit that was true. It was another element of ambiguity that made the whole thing fuzzier, more tangled, convoluted, and weird.

That - the nagging, anxious but reasonable doubt - was the context of what came next. And, innocent or guilty, reasonable doubt should always be on my side, right?

# Chapter Fourteen

## The Delusions that Haunt Me

It got more complicated during my regular Wednesday night shift. More cereal boxes. More coffee and tea and iced tea and flavoured water-like beverages and mindless carrying, stacking, arranging, and rotating. I was using box cutters to break down a big carton when she recognized me.

"Oh, hey, you're the guy from the gym," she said. "You were asking about Don." I don't normally do gymnasiums, so it took me a moment to process the reference. It was the person who worked at the athletic centre, the one who'd told me about Big Don's ambition.

"Oh. Yeah. Right. Hi."

"It's great, isn't it?"

"What's great?"

"You haven't heard? That's right, I didn't exactly recommend him, did I - you hired someone else?"

"I didn't end up hiring anyone. And thanks again for the heads up," I said, seeing no reason to make anything up. "Did something good happen?"

"Big Don. Got his investment and he's on his way to his dream job. Royal Caravelle Cruises, here he comes."

"Oh. That's ... good for him I guess."

"Anyway, I just wondered if you were one of the ones who helped him out."

"Me, no. As you can see, I'm not exactly in a position to invest much."

"Just as well - I hope his investors see their money back. Don is mostly just into Don." Again, it must have been my gormless face, the face that screams harmlessness.

"Right," I said in a casually worldly way, hiding the panic I was beginning to feel.

Big Don got his money?

From ... Mom?

It was the ghost of Gary. Defend the home, my instincts screamed, rescue The Plan, our lives! But I was paralyzed by the lack of options. What was I supposed to do? I had used all my credit with Mom - my input in the matter was more than unwelcome. I couldn't go to the cops and accuse Don of doing something he hadn't done yet. I couldn't even confront *him* about it. My mind was a blank.

I existed for a couple of days in a soft-focus, white-noised haze as I oozed from one everyday task to the next. Mom didn't notice because she was working so much. At school they probably chalked it up to my artistic personality - must have been in the funk of creative ennui.

Amy had called me delusional. She meant irrational, but I'm not the one to correct her. Didn't someone famous once remark that we all need our delusions just to get through the day?

Or maybe that was me.

According to the biology types, adults think and reason with their prefrontal cortex. Teenagers, like me, rely on the amygdala, more of a hunch-inducing-feeling kinda place. Now either my reason or my (Amy would say) delusions were telling me that I had to deal with Don before things got out of hand. If Mom figured that she'd been scammed, who knows what might happen? Being out some cash would be bad, sure. But there were other issues. Both my gut and my brain were figuring that once a person kills their first slimeball, the second might not be so hard. A person might not require as much provocation.

This called for thinking and planning and then planning and thinking. In my defence, that is what I did to the exclusion of just about anything else. Except eating and sleeping. A brain needs fuel and rest. And Netflix. A brain needs some distraction.

I devised a strategy based on the resources at my disposal and attempted a timely intervention. First I needed information. I had to find out if Mom had given this guy any money. So, given that she was working twelve-hour shifts, and using my knowledge of her passwords, I got to work. The first thing I found in her banking records was an e-transfer of three thousand dollars.

Shit.

That might not seem like a lot of money to some people, but to us, to me, to The Plan it was huge. Six months' pay to me. For Mom, it was her share of my first-year tuition at animation college. So not only would I not get to go, it was an added sentence of several months' labour at the Grocery Barn.

Even if Big Don was telling the truth, it wasn't the sort of gamble that Mom would normally make. She was desperate for the extra cash and I didn't know why. I couldn't find any hint of a reason in financial records, emails, or texts. I was going to have to get it out of Mom, but that was liable to be a big argument about my place in the family hierarchy.

This was no time to argue.

I had to get the money back.

I had to save The Plan.

Besides, Don might not like what I was going to do, but it might save his life.

# Chapter Fifteen

## Impersonating My Mother Is the Creepiest Thing I've Ever Done

In the morning I borrowed Mom's phone when she was in the shower. I looked through a few messages to make sure I wouldn't mess up her messaging voice. She didn't have any bizarre texting disabilities and mostly just said things in short phrases, so I think I did a fair impersonation. Still, it made me intensely uncomfortable. I found Don's number and I fired a text his way, hoping that he was an early riser, being such a healthy and fit kinda guy.

**Me** (trying to sound Mom-ish): Hey, Don, can I see you tonight? Just for a short talk.

This was all going to blow up if Don didn't see this or didn't want to answer or was totally ghosting her now that he had her money. He took forever to reply. I waited for two agonizing minutes.

**Don**: Anything for you, girl. Where and when?

I wanted to puke. Do men still talk to women that way?

**Me**: Not here. Teenager issues. And car's in the shop, so can I meet you at Rideau Station?
**Don**: I can pick you up. If ya know what I mean. Ha Ha.
**Me**: No worries. Rideau Station at 8:00. OK?

**Don**: Sure. See ya.

I quickly deleted the exchange. I carefully put the phone where I found it but turned it off. With any luck, if he texted again, Mom wouldn't know and she'd be at work most of the day, where her phone was turned off all the time. It was risky and I had a long, nervous day. I had to hope that Don kept the date and didn't text her ahead of time to change things. All I could do was move toward the fraudulent rendezvous, cool and calm and in control.

I did my school work, looked after the dog, fed myself leftovers, and chose my skulking wardrobe - a nondescript hoodie and jeans. I got on the number 51 bus to get to the nearest LRT station, paid cash and grabbed a transfer - no record of my trip would appear on my smart transit card. At Tunney's Pasture, I boarded the LRT and rode standing, looking out the window preparing for my meeting with Big Don.

I considered running this all by Amy - discussing the ins and outs of my plan. Not a good idea. No matter how much I worshipped Amy, I was not going to let her tell me what to do right now. She'd be telling me to let Mom look after herself, not to interfere. Amy didn't realize that any threat to The Plan *is* my business.

Consider this - any day now, any MINUTE now, Amy would realize that I am and would continue to be a waste of time. Because she's a nice person, she wouldn't outright dump me, but she'd just stop texting, stop meeting with me, we'll drift apart like people do, especially when one of them is perfect and gorgeous and the other is me. All I had was The Plan. I had to keep my eye on the prize.

I also had to keep my eye out for the sporty personality and kinesthetic glow of Big Don. I had the advantage because he wouldn't know who I am. I'd get there early, so I'd be able to watch the platforms as well as the entrances. I'd gambled that he'd probably be coming from the west, like me and I stayed on the platform waiting and watching.

The scene was clear in my head and I rehearsed several versions. They all began with a cautious, non-threatening approach.

"You're here to meet someone?" I'd say.

"Excuse me?" He'd reply, or maybe he'd just look at me vacantly.

"Kelly Martel. She's not coming."

"Who are you?"

"I'm her son, the one whose tuition you want to borrow, or maybe steal so that you can get your cruise ship gig."

"What are you talking about? I'm not stealing anything."

"Right - it's an investment scam."

"Listen, kid, you don't …"

"Don't call me kid. I'm here to get the money back."

"You'll get your money back. When it's time."

"No, I think I'll be having it back right now."

"Really? And just how do you think you're gonna do that?"

"Easy - I just go to the cruise company, Royal Caravelle, and tell them about how you like to bilk women out of their savings. That you're a con man, a grifter, out to exploit the easy marks they send your way. They might not be so keen on having you around their passengers when they find out."

"That's blackmail. And completely false. No one is bilking anyone of anything!"

"Great - prove it - give my mother her money back. Do what you have to do - sell your shitbox truck, rob a bank, sell a kidney. I don't care."

"You get nothing from me - you and your mother are both trash. Desperate, stupid trash."

I had to be careful - somewhere in here, my frozen ball of rage might express itself. It wasn't the sort of thing I had any experience controlling. I tried to consider an appropriately sarcastic remark when my fantasy came crashing in upon me. I couldn't think of anything to say. All I had was anger. Fierce frozen righteous rage at this guy I wasn't even talking to, anger about a conversation I had imagined.

There was a blur of activity. Lights. White noise. Screams. Shouts. Alarms, then running feet, more shouts.

And sirens. A lot of sirens.

Big Don, it turns out, would be famous.

The first person killed on Ottawa's new LRT.

So, I was out of luck. I guess Don was, too.

# Chapter Sixteen

## Normally I *Like* Pushing Buttons

They thought he fell in front of a train.

Mom found out about Big Don's dive on the same day that the police found out that she and Don had gone on a few dates. Which was early the next morning. They worked surprisingly fast sometimes.

That night at Rideau Station, I had run for cover as soon as the panicked activity started.  I flew up the stairs and what must be one of the longest escalators in the universe to the exit and ran to a bus stop to try to get home. The trains were likely to be offline for a while. I wasn't sure what I'd seen, let alone what happened. It was all a confusion of sound and light mixed with an overdose of whatever brain drug makes your hands shake and your throat tighten. I had a bruise on my arm, but I got that at work, and otherwise I was fine physically. I made it home to lie awake in bed for what seemed like days waiting for the sound of my mother to return. When I heard her come in I relaxed a bit but was still unable to shake the effects of my confusion.

Should I tell Mom about trying to meet with Don? No good came of it - he still had our money and we were never ever getting it back. Not now. Should I ask her where she was, and, by the way, did she push Don in front of the train?

And what had made me run like that? I could have stayed to try and help, maybe figured out what had happened.

No. No way.

I think I saw him there, but I hadn't talked to him.

But if I were to be interviewed by police, they would put my picture up on their whiteboard titled, "Loser Suspects," subtitled, "No Alibi."

I'm thinking about the cops because, of course, here they were, at our house, interviewing Mom for the third time. After a sleepless night, I'd heard them pull up and raced into my eavesdropping hidey-hole behind the basement door.

I noticed their tone right away, the one that said, "It's only reasonable for everyone to think you killed the guy, am I right?" First, they told Mom what had happened at Rideau Station. Again, she didn't seem overly shocked or upset. I couldn't help but think that no matter what, she should try to sound more surprised or something. She just came across cold. Maybe that's why the detectives took the tone they did.

"So it's just coincidence that these two men are dead." I guess there was an added layer of sarcasm if they suspected you of not one but two murders. That was the woman from before. I found out her name was Detective Sergeant Tremblay. She was tag-teaming with Reynolds again.

"How would I know?" Mom said calmly.

"It's what you'd like us to think, isn't it? One just happens to have his eye drops tampered with. The other just happens to jump in front of a train."

"I doubt that either of those things *just* happens."

Silence from the detectives.

"You think I date men a few times and then murder them ... maybe because they tell me I should smile more?"

Yes! Good one!

"Did you have contact with Mr. Buckley yesterday?" asked Reynolds.

"I'm sure you know I did."

What? She did? Wait - that was a good thing. The cops would have his phone, they'd have seen the texts I sent.

"What was the nature of your contact?"

"I'm sure you know that, too. I had lent him some money and I wanted to get it back. I texted him and I talked to him."

"When you say money - hundreds?"

"Three thousand." I imagined them writing the number on their pads.

"Okay, so, you asked him for the money back, and he said no problem?"

"He said he'd spent it, and that I'd have to wait." There was silence then as if everyone was letting the implications of that settle.

"And this conversation happened just before Mr. Buckley was killed. Isn't that interesting."

"A conversation on the phone, thank you." Mom didn't wait to be asked anything else, but spoke up to say, "And if you think that was upsetting for me, maybe consider how I feel now - now that Don is dead, that money is gone forever."

More silence. Then, The Great Detective sighed and asked, "If you can clear up where you were last night - it would mean a lot to me."

"I was out."

Wow. You had to hand it to her. Ice in her veins.

"Out where, please," Sergeant Tremblay said flatly.

"Out ... with a man for a drink ... at a bar."

"And did this man meet with any accidents since you saw him?"

"Details, please, Ms. Martel," Reynolds said quickly before Mom could react to Tremblay's provocation.

"Mike Lawrence. A pub in the market called The White Hart. From about eight."

"So ... from about the time Mr. Buckley found himself face to face with a train."

"Is it some sort of crime to be the last person someone talked to?"

"We didn't say that. Is that what you think?"

"I have no idea."

"And when did you get home?"

"I dunno - maybe ten, ten-thirty."

"If you'll give us the contact information for Mr. Lawrence?" Tremblay demanded.

Mom looked on her phone and they recorded the number.

"We'll be checking this out, just so you know," said Reynolds as he stuffed his notebook in his pocket.

"Knock yourselves out."

Again with the ice. Mom has stones. So to speak.

"Just one more thing. I hope you don't mind," said Reynolds, using a ploy he'd probably learned from TV. "Chase's father, David Robinson, where is he now?"

There was a long pause and Mom sighed.

"I don't know. He disappeared a long time ago."

"Did you look for him?" asked Tremblay.

"Nope."

"And why was that?" asked Reynolds.

"You're the detective. Look at the court documents."

"Oh, we have, Ms. Martel," said Reynolds. "We just wanted to hear it from you."

"It's all in the report and it doesn't have anything to do with anything. I was a ... a victim then, and so was my son, and you're not making another victim of me or him now."

I couldn't see what they were doing, but in my mind the two detectives looked at each other and then back at Mom, assessing her in that way cops have, weighing her words against what they knew and also against what they could infer from her non-verbal behaviour. The last thing they did was ask Mom if she ever wore a hat. They had probably been looking around the house for one, just to catch her in a lie. Mom's not a hat person, though she might borrow one from me on rainy days. I heard them say something about being in touch and then the front door closed with its familiar shudder.

I was fairly bursting with questions when I came out from behind the door. I could see the stress in the way Mom's arms were crossed and in the set of her jaw. I gave her an awkward one-armed hug.

"So Big Don's dead? That's ... awful." I was as incredulous as I could manage.

"Apparently. And we're out three thousand dollars, as I'm sure you heard." She stressed that last phrase a little pointedly, like I was the one who had done something wrong.

"So you went on a date after work last night?" I asked casually.

"Not really a ... date," she sighed.

"Then what was it?"

Silence.

"None of my business?" I asked.

More silence. I sat down at the kitchen table and Mom started to make coffee. About time. I was dying here without my morning caffeine blast.

"Will the guy back you up?"

"No idea - he's not the sort who will enjoy being questioned by the cops. If they can track him down. I got the impression he's shy."

"Doesn't sound like much of a date."

"Look, I just answered all kinds of questions from the cops, and I don't need to be given the third degree by you." I just stared at her, silently asking her to answer anyway.

"Let's just say I had to talk to him about something. It doesn't concern you."

Yeah, right. I didn't say anything about the money because the shock of that had worn off yesterday. Maybe that was a mistake. From her point of view, I should have been alarmed. But there was another point the cops had made which interested me more.

"Okay, what was all that about Whatshisname? Court records?"

"Yeah - there are court records. You don't want to see them. It'll just make you unhappy. I told you he was a piece of work. I told you he was violent. I got the police involved, for all the good it did."

She poured us both coffee and retreated to the living room couch where Loki was waiting for her, his belly exposed for a scratch. Everything from her tone of voice to the way she sat down told me to let it go, that she was near the end of her rope. I didn't follow but made some toast and then went to my room to get a little mental space.

All sorts of buttons in my mind had been pushed, all kinds of subroutines activated. Creative ones (I was writing my own backstory, filling in details about my early life, and boy, did the lighting just change), apprehensive ones (the cops are probably thinking Mom's responsible for

THREE murders now), and self-involved post-Millennial ones (Daddy was a violent creep, Mommy and Murder both start with M, and I'm ... a walking candidate for a serious dissociative disorder).

Each of those three functions required serious teenage headspace. Chase needed Chase time to think Chase thoughts. When I was able to accommodate everything I'd have to get another perspective to make sure I wasn't becoming completely unhinged.

I needed Amy.

Or maybe Rich or Carter first, to get some less critical, less demanding feedback.

Yeah - shallow end of the pool before the deep end.

Rich and Carter before Amy, too.

# Chapter Seventeen
## The Best Questions Are Always the Ones No One Asks

The basement of the Maa'ingan family house was one of our regular meeting places. Carter has a semi-finished TV room down there with a big sectional couch. He, Rich, and I all had our phones out and we showed each other Instagram posts and YouTube videos. It was one of the ways we'd spend lunch breaks, getting away from the gloomy brick of our ancient high school.

I figured that it was a good time to bring up a couple of things, especially because we all had to be back in class in forty minutes. If they thought I was insane, their abuse wouldn't last long.

"So, have you guys ever wondered what happened to my dad?"

Neither of them said anything.

"Seriously, have you ever wondered what happened to him?"

Carter was the first to figure out something to say. "Why are you asking *us*?"

"Because I want to know what you think."

"What we think ... about what?" asked Rich. "It's kind of none of our business."

"Don't you think it's strange that no one has ever heard from him, that he's never tried to make contact?"

"Like Rich said - none of our business. What do *you* think?"

"I think it's pretty weird. He's got no digital footprint that I can find, he's not registered as a missing person, there's no warrant for his arrest, he's not been declared legally dead, nothing. But he's never made contact."

"I thought you'd given him up as permanently disappeared years ago. You never, and I mean literally *never*, talk about him." Carter stuffed his phone in his pocket, something he only did if he was actually interested in something.

So, I laid it out for them. GareBear. Big Don. The cops interrogating Mom. And the fact that they were asking about my father. I put it all in the context of what the detectives might be suspicious about, trying not to point to any conclusions that I might have thought were obvious. I left out the fact that I was at Rideau Station when Don was killed.

"And if you're a cop, what do you do if you think that a guy falling in front of a train might be suspicious?"

"You look at the security camera recordings," Carter said immediately.

"Right. So, if they've got it all on video, why are they interviewing my mother at all?"

"Maybe they don't have it on video," Rich said. "Bad angles, obscured view ...."

"Or the cameras weren't working at all. But it means that they have questions about why Don fell in front of a train."

"Holy shit," Rich said softly.

"Exactly, the shit that is holy," I replied.

"They think your mother is some kind of black widow?"

"That's insane, right?" I needed to be the one who said it. I'd be able to read their thoughts in their reactions.

"Totally," said Rich.

"Yeah, yeah. Absolutely," said Carter.

They were both lying. Their faces told me as well as the two things that happened next.

There was an uncomfortable pause and then Rich changed the subject.

"Speaking of insane, I have to meet Émilie's grandmother tonight." Émilie was Rich's latest girlfriend. Carter and I looked at him, both silently asking for more information.

"She only speaks French!"

"Oooooh," we sang together. We weren't being sarcastic. A triple whammy - family, a generation gap, and now anglophone awkwardness. Given the number of things that were embarrassing about simply existing in proximity to a girlfriend's family, language problems were a mad, bad minefield.

"I don't know," Carter began, "maybe do what you know best - just smile and nod, don't say anything and laugh when everyone else laughs."

"Good advice," I affirmed. "Be the strong, silent, yet affable type. But make eye contact with Granny. She'll think that's good."

"Yeah, right. And if you do have to talk, smile and keep it short," Carter continued.

"Good - yeah. I can do that. That's what I need - some rules. Eye contact, smile and keep it short."

That was the same advice I'd give anyone being interviewed by the police, a situation I never thought I'd be in, but one that was likely to happen again. Fairly soon. Best to be prepared. It helps if you're actually telling the truth, of course, but the big ideas are the same. Build trust, and keep your answers short.

We picked up our stuff and headed up the stairs and out the door. Buoyed by our advice, Rich could face the rest of the day with less anxiety if not actual confidence. I would have felt a little more sympathy for him had I not been preparing for my own engagement with destiny.

I'd had my rehearsal. My story made a certain amount of sense. It wasn't insane. With some added detail, and perhaps a little editorial embellishment, I might soon place the facts in front of Amy.

And she would slay me.

But it had to be done.

# Chapter Eighteen

## Monster Killer Zombie Dad

I approached my next task, to convince Amy, with clarity. When I mentioned offhand that I thought I knew what happened to Don, she looked shocked. Then, when my hypothesis became clear, her tone changed.

"Honestly. You are such a creep."

"What? Why?"

"You seem to be ready to accept that your mother is a cold-blooded killer. With no evidence. First, she protected baby YOU from your father and raised you alone. She works and scrapes and saves for your future. She has the bad luck to meet a manipulative creep like Gary, but she realizes her mistake and throws him out. Remember how much you despised him? You should be standing between her and the cops, you should be shouting abuse, demanding warrants, calling lawyers, all that stuff you learn by watching TV."

"My semi-coherent answers were enough to throw the cops off until Big Don screwed things up. It really got them going when they found out that Mom knew him. You should have heard the suspicion in the detectives' voices. They practically accused her of killing TWO more people - Whatshisname *and* the guy she was with last week when Big Don died."

"They do that to shake everyone up. It clearly worked on you. You've lost your mind."

"And she wouldn't tell me what she was meeting this other guy about." I made a mental note to find out more about that meeting. It would either answer some questions or help me figure out what steps I might need to take next to protect Mom.

"Maybe because it's none of your business. And now you're taking the absence of information as an admission of guilt. Your imagination is taking over your higher functions. You're not thinking, you're script-writing."

"It's not a script if it's the only series of deductions that works."

"Wait a minute - she was on the phone with him just before he died. *On the phone*. She wasn't there and the phone records will prove it."

"They might prove she was on the phone, but she could have been standing right behind him. At Rideau Station or in the market, it's gonna be the same cellphone tower." That made her stop and think for a minute.

"I can think of other storylines that fit the facts."

"Like what?"

"Like ... Your dad's not dead. He disappeared fifteen years ago and has come back. He kills both Gary and Don, satisfying a cold, jealous rage as well as a need to get revenge."

"Revenge? On who?"

"On your mother, dope. He sets her up so that she goes to jail. Even better, he can return ... and kill YOU." She poked her index finger into my breastbone.

"Me? Why kill me? What did I ever do?"

"You came along and spoiled everything, remember? He's been seething with murderous anger for fifteen years, moving from petty crime to petty crime, biding his time and sharpening his plan. Setting your mother up for your murder will be easy if the cops think she's already murdered two others. She goes to jail for, like, EVER, and he just melts away and crawls back under a rock to die. And so, too, dies any chance your mother will have of proving her innocence."

"Cool."

"No, not cool - ridiculous. Asinine. Like you."

"Wait - how did he plant the eye drops? How did he even know to do that?"

"That's not the point!"

"But it is. Your version is not as credible as mine."

"Mine has motive - yours just relies on the idea that everybody had to hate Gary as much as you did. You think everyone had a motive."

"That's IT!"

"What is?"

"Everyone *does* have a motive. It's brilliant! The only people who don't realize that are the people who never met Gary. The cops have to discover a motive, something they can relate to before they can hang his death on somebody specific. Remember we don't know how Gary got his money, what all of his late-night meetings were about. The cops will look elsewhere when they realize it was Gary's purpose in life to help acquaintances discover their potential as murderers."

"Why is it brilliant?"

"Because, Mom, or me, or even you are in the clear because we don't have a motive more convincing than anyone else. For us, the time to kill him would surely have been earlier, when we could have faked it better - no need for eye drops with peanut sauce."

"Don't bring me into this. It makes me sick just to think about it."

"There is a killer in all of us. Some of us just need better reasons than others."

"What has made you so dark lately?"

"I'm just thinking about people and their casual indifference to each other."

"Casual indifference? What brought this on?"

That was my in. I showed her.

# Chapter Nineteen

## Monster Killer Spandex Dude

*Silent Killer, member-in-good-standing of the Urban Predators, effortlessly pumps the cranks of his ultra-lite bike. Just the commuting bike today, but with carbon frame, tubeless tires. And hydraulic brakes, not that he used them much. He smiles as he jets down the recreational pathway, thighs feeling full, massaged by their spandex stockings, knees feeling stronger with every pump, making the best time of the week. Rounding a long curve near the river, he sees the opportunity ahead.*

*The path is his. It belongs to whoever takes ownership, to whoever is the biggest, fastest, the most deserving of its velvety ribbon of asphalt. And Silent Killer is deserving. Highly practiced, even more highly skilled. Brain, bone, muscle, and bike perfectly synced.*

*Obstacles are opportunities to demonstrate speed, precision handling, and ownership.*

*A woman. Two kids.*

*(POV switches to see Silent Killer approaching from a distance and we see and hear the little family interacting on their morning outing. Then back to his view from between the handlebars.)*

*Tiny people, tiny bikes, no sense of appropriate speed, lacking the courtesy to immediately get out of His Way. And ahead of them, some other guy, probably a nobody teenager.*

*Not a problem.*

*No need for a call of warning.*

*No need for a bell. Not that he had one.*

*He is the wind on wheels. He blows past one, two, three. The teenager has removed himself from the path. He has stopped and watches Silent Killer jet past.*

*And he is alone once more, one with bike and path until he reaches and overcomes the next obstacle. And the next. And so it goes until he dismounts at the bike stand outside the tall grey and glass office complex that is his goal. He loosens his helmet, detaches the front wheel, double locks everything else. He turns to enter his building and feels more than sees another cyclist approaching.*

*A high-pitched bell sounds. He turns left to see the rider gliding towards him. He doesn't notice anything about the oncoming cyclist except for the sunglasses. They are large, dark, yet mirrored.*

*He sees himself in the glasses, sees himself from the point of view of a tiny child on a tiny bike as a monstrous man races past in the blink of an eye, his wake knocking the boy onto the ground. There is hurt, and crying, but mostly shock and fear, and the feeling that he never wants to ride a bike again.*

*The boy would get over it.*

*But Silent Killer would not.*


"Is this a novel?"

"No - you know I'm no good with words - it's the first phase of a screenplay."

"I know you're no good with drawing. You're plenty good with words. Where's the dialogue?"

"There isn't any."

"So it's a silent movie?"

"Nooo. There will be - this is just the first scene, before any backstory, before we see who anybody is, before we get to the conflict and the stakes."

Amy frowned as her eyes scanned the last few lines. "The glasses thing - I thought you said there would be no superpowers."

"It's not a power like that. It's a presence, an attitude, a worldly glance kind of thing that makes people have some insight into their own crapulence."

She put the page down on the coffee table and patted it. "And how is it funny?"

"That's where the animation comes in - the whole scene where he's ripping around is full of comic potential and it's only the final vision that lets both the character and the audience know what a total shit he is. Later in the movie, we cut to a scene where he's too afraid to get on his bike - it'll write itself."

"Okay ... Now you have to figure out why any of it matters."

If that seems like faint praise, it's not. For Amy that was big - the questions stopped after only a handful and I had an answer for every one of them.

I must have been beaming at her because she reined me in. "Seems to me a worse punishment would be to just let him go on like that until he can look back on it in late middle-age and realize what a shit he's been his whole life."

She laughed - at me or with me, I didn't know.

I was busy thinking about it - if someone went through life so completely oblivious, so utterly un-self-aware, what sort of monster would they be in mid-life?

Was THAT what Gary had been?

And Big Don?

Was Mom just doing what my protagonist couldn't, taking predators off the streets?

Go, Mom!

# Chapter Twenty

## Monster Killer Hot Mom?

The media were going nuts. How could the new LRT be running without adequate security cameras? A man had died and we didn't know why. Would the plague of slowdowns and letdowns, the sinkhole of glitches, failures, and foibles ever be resolved? How many people would have to die? And what about the children? Who will speak for the *children*?

Okay, I made up that last part but the point was that no one seemed to know why Big Don ended up in pieces down on those tracks. Personally, I figured that the cops had way more information than they let on.

And maybe someone else knew, but she wasn't saying anything.

We were actually going through a period of significantly reduced communication at my house. Unspoken questions circled the room above our heads. Lies and half-truths were prepared and nurtured as if time and care could make them real.

Because I am an amazing son, I'd make her toast and coffee before work and while doing so I did not ask her any questions about the money she had "invested" in Big Don. And as we ate, I didn't ask her why she was willing to risk her savings, and then, between bites, why she needed the return he promised.

Because she is a good mother, she made me dinner unless she was working, and she'd mince ginger and chop onions for curry, and while doing so didn't ask me why I hadn't asked her those first two questions - it had to be on her mind, but she didn't want to bring it up. Over dessert, which we almost never ate, she also didn't ask me where *I* was the night

Don died. She probably didn't want to come on like she was suspicious of me, which she had every right to be, of course, given how suspicious I was of her. There were some uncomfortable questions to be asked and answered.

I was washing dishes. Mom was drying and putting away. "So, the other night, "she began. "Don seemed to be under the impression that I was meeting him at Rideau Station. Why would he think that?"

I felt the blood run out of my face and I half-turned away so that she wouldn't see. "How would I know?"

"He said I texted him early in the morning."

"So you texted him. Who cares?"

"But I didn't. Text him."

"I guess you guys got your wires crossed."

"Robinson, did you use my phone to text Don? Were you trying … something?"

And I did my best to be like she was with the detectives, to have ice water in my veins, to lie with utter clarity. Or better - tell the truth and make it sound like a lie. "Right, Kelly. I impersonate you on your phone. Next you'll be telling me that I dress up in your clothes to go meet men."

"I can't protect you if you do stupid things."

"Like you protected me from Whatshisname?" I stressed the last word and looked her in the eye, going on offence before the conversation got even more uncomfortable. It was time to bring up what Amy had said about enraged killer zombie dad.

"What do you mean?"

"Amy said something funny the other day." Mom liked Amy. If I started off with her, I was likely to get a more charitable audience.

"Don't change the subject."

"I'm not. We, me and Amy, were talking about Gary, and about being interviewed by the police, and going over what they might be thinking."

"Right. Her dad's a Crown prosecutor, isn't he?"

"He is?"

"Come on. Are you telling me you didn't know?"

"I remember the Crown part …. But anyway, just for fun, Amy made up a story about how Whatshisname maybe has come out of hiding and murdered Gary and Don in a jealous rage." She stopped drying a wooden bowl and looked at me.

"That *is* funny. In a very dark way."

"And completely ridiculous, right?"

"Yes."

She said it like it was a conclusion. Not good enough.

"How? How is it ridiculous?"

"In any number of ways."

I scrubbed the last piece of cooked rice off the bottom of a large silver pot. "Humour me."

Then there was a big sigh. "Chase, …."

"Mom?"

"Your father could not be running around murdering people."

"How about lurching?"

"No, not … that either."

"Why not?"

Another sigh.

"He's dead."

"You mean you think he's dead."

"No. He's dead."

"If you knew that, you would have told me before now."

"I only just found out a while ago - for sure, I mean."

Those first questions had come to me fairly easily, as I had been preparing to ask them for a long time. But this last bit of information - the colours in my world shifted a bit. A little richer, A little darker.

Mom switched on the kettle to begin making herself herbal tea while I figured out how to respond.

"How is that possible? He disappeared fifteen years ago."

"Sit down."

And it all came out, with lots of Kelly pauses. Behind the curtain of our mundane lives, Mom had some secrets. Big ones. First, though, it was no secret that when I was about two, my parents' marriage was toast. Mom had reported Dad to the police. Amy's ridiculous scenario had one detail right - he was in an overwhelming, constant, jealous rage. She was scared of him, scared that he would hurt her, scared that he would take me.

And then one day he did. Take me.

Today, they'd issue an Amber Alert on everyone's radio and cellphone but there was no such thing then. Moreover, dear ol' Whatshisname had left Mom a message, and she knew where he'd taken me and he'd made it clear that if he saw the police, he'd kill us both. He was in the headspace of murder-suicide and Mom didn't know what option she had but to try and talk him out of it. She said she knew that she'd probably be victim number one, but that she needed to go and take care of me.

So, by herself, without anyone in the world to know or help, she borrowed a friend's car and drove an hour and a half to a place we'd been to as a family south of town, a place where the rock of the Shield poked through and the terrain was rugged and treed and wild. My so-called father had clearly chosen it to be isolated so that he could control his little final act with all the narcissistic drama he could muster. She found us and comforted an exhausted, crying me, and put me in a carrier on her back and followed psycho-dad into the woods where she thought that if she died that night, at least she was giving me a chance that I wouldn't have had otherwise.

As she talked, my cinematic imagination filled in her many narrative oversights. Whatshisname jabbered on and on, his paranoid, jealous obsessions, his professions of love, his refusal to accept responsibility for his own crappy life growing in weirdness and volume. On Mom's back in the carrier, I had been rocked to sleep, my head lolling to one side.

Suddenly, he stopped. They had been climbing for a short time and as he halted and turned to face her, Mom could see nothing behind him. A void. A black pit. His voice choking with conviction, he'd narrow his eyes, beseeching understanding, and he would tell Mom why he brought us there, why he had to kill us all.

Of course, it was because he loved us so much.

She didn't let him get far. In my mind, she pummeled him with both fists, right, left and then right again until he took a step backwards to protect himself. As he began to move, she bent her knees and shoved him up and back with all her strength. He stumbled, regaining his balance briefly until she pushed again, harder, using her legs, shoulders and arms to maximize her leverage. They were at the apex of a rocky outcropping and this time he went over the edge, arms and fingers clawing at the air, dropping five or ten metres. There would have been a thump, maybe two and then the near silence of the forest at night, wind in the treetops and crickets gently chirping. That's what I heard in my head, anyway.

She told me she didn't know how far he'd fallen or care to see if he survived. All she could think about was escape. He probably never regained consciousness, died of exposure that night.

She hurried back to the road and drove home.

I did what I could at the time to help. I slept.

And Mom waited for a knock on the door. Waited for the police to tell her the news. Waited for an autopsy to reveal the method of his death and for the police to return.

But none of that happened. He'd left his car a long way away, must have hitched a ride with someone the police never knew about, maybe using me as some kind of sympathy card with a passing driver. I couldn't tell anyone anything. My two-year-old's perceptions were pretty much what you'd expect. He'd covered his own tracks, so Mom didn't have to cover hers. No one looked for him, because no one knew he was there.

Until Gary.

And Gary only looked for him because he knew where to go. Mom is not a drinker and one night she reminded herself why. In a moment of wine-fueled candour, she had told her story to Gary Twolan, who was just the sort of person to go have a look for himself, to mark the spot where he found the rotted remains and to carefully pin the location in his GPS.

Gary was not interested in justice, or the respectful treatment of a corpse. Gary was interested in blackmail, and for what he thought Mom could do for him.

# Chapter Twenty-One

## Three Motives for Murder Is Enough for Most People

"Look at this parasite."

I spoke in low tones, not that he'd hear us.

"Millennial Man is probably into his third hour." A phone and a laptop were on the table in front of him beside his long-empty latté. Two chargers connected to the wall receptacle to his right. To his left, his long legs and size twelve Blundstones stretched to infinity. His jacket was on the chair opposite him. Dark glasses prevented passersby from making eye contact, and earbuds enclosed him in an envelope of sound.

"What about him?"

"Look at this place." I gestured to the scene in the coffee shop. The barista is sending clouds of steam into the air as the serving line in front of him lengthens almost to the exit. Customers with coffee, hats, gloves in their hand scan for seating and wait for the next available chair in the small archipelago of tables. Moms juggle hot drinks and babies, staff swirling to serve, clean, and assist, short grey heads with walkers manoeuvering to find a place to sit. "Someone should get him to shift his parasitic ass." Amy and I got up and offered our seats, swallowing the last of our coffees in big gulps.

"Sure, he's annoying, self-involved, and oblivious, but so what?" Amy was always too ready to accept people's faults.

"Why does the world put up with that, with people who are too dense to perceive themselves?" I complained.

"Maybe he's worth it. Maybe he has good qualities."

"Doubt it."

"We are all mixed bags. Despite your overall okayness, you, for example, have an unforgiving and suspicious mind. But everyone has positive qualities. I bet even Gary had something good in his personality."

"Gary - both parasite and predator," I said shaking my head.

"Predator?"

"Big time."

"What have you found out? What do you know?" She grabbed my arm and pulled me back to face her as we left the coffee shop. "Gary was threatening your mom, wasn't he?"

"I can't tell you."

"You can't tell anyone if Gary was threatening your mom?"

"No - I can't tell *you*."

"Make sense, please." She stood right in front of me, nose to nose, and looked at me with those eyes, those ponds of green stuff that could unlock my every thought and deepest feelings in about five seconds. She had power that she did not understand.

"Because of who your dad is - a Crown prosecutor." And the eyes widened.

"You think I'll tell him? No way. This is your mother we're talking about. Besides, he tells me nothing about his work and I tell *him* nothing about his work."

So I caved. It's what I wanted to do all along, but I needed to be able to tell myself that she'd forced it out of me. We sat on a bench on the corner opposite the coffee shop and I told her the story, and her eyes grew wider, and her expression more intense, and she kept saying, "*Ohmygod.*"

I stopped talking to let everything sink in, almost as much for me as for her. It always surprises me that telling a story helps me understand it better than I ever would if I just heard or read it. I could see it better now - Mom keeping the secret long enough to convince herself that she no longer had a choice, that the longer she waited, the more it looked like she was covering things up. She would have lost me in about three minutes to foster care and then potentially spent years in jail. I wondered if the fact that I was older now made her relax just enough to allow her to tell Gary in a moment of weakness.

Amy snapped me out of my inner roaming. "So, he literally knew where the body is hidden."

"Yeah - and he was finding out how far Mom would go to keep it a secret. When she finally kicked him out he was both threatening me and demanding that she steal from her client - a rich old lady with more than enough money and just enough dementia to make it worth ripping her off."

One final, "*Ohmygod,*" and she said, "No one can ever know - they'll think she killed him for sure. It's not one motive but three."

"Tell me about it. I don't sound so delusional now, do I?"

"Have you gone to get them yet?"

"Get what?"

"Your dad's bones!"

"Could you maybe not yell stuff like that in public?"

"Sorry." Then, more quietly, she added, "If the cops have all of Gary's things, they might look into his phone long and hard enough to investigate why he pinned a location in the bush a couple of months before he died. Gary was not an outdoors person. They might think it's suspicious, or significant." She reached across the table and grabbed my arm. "You can't let them find those remains."

"Shit." I hadn't thought of that. "Forget it - going into the bush, finding the bones of my father who had tried to kill me and my mother, and then bringing them out and hiding them somewhere is absolutely the last thing I want to do. Not on my day off, anyway."

"But you have to! It's the least you can do."

"No, the least I can do is nothing, and I've already shown I'm willing to do more than that."

"As long as those remains are there, your mother could be charged with manslaughter at the least - and who knows - Gary might have shared his scam with someone else. She's still vulnerable to blackmail."

"I don't even know where they are."

"Your mom does and if Gary could find them, so can we."

"We?"

"Yes - I'm coming."

"But that'll make you an accessory, won't it? If things go bad?"

"Why would they go bad? Besides, technically, as soon as you told me I was an accessory, so I'm willing to take the chance."

"She won't let us do it."

"Don't tell her - just get the location from her and we'll do the rest."

Amy was strangely energized by the idea of an expedition into the forest to find a body. Maybe it was because she hadn't had much of a chance to think it through and figure out the morbidly gross and stinky details, but her eyes were wide with excitement as she leaned forward as if itching to jump into action. It was like she'd been waiting to go for a walk on the wild side, and this would do for a start.

So, if things went well, I'd get to hang out for a day with Amy, help prevent further blackmail of my mother while collecting the remains of my long-dead homicidal father.

How could I say no?

# Chapter Twenty-Two

## GareBear Bait

Our small living room couch that matches everything and nothing. The air heavy and close with things we were both refusing to say.

"Why do you want to know?" she asked.

"Because it's my right."

"How do you figure that?"

"Because I was there even if I was only two and it happened to me and I want to KNOW."

"But there's no reason to. It'll just bother you, especially if you're ever near there."

"It's bothering me now. And Gary knew. It's more than bothering me that Gary knew something about me that I don't. Haunting me, *tormenting* me. You get the idea."

No, I didn't tell her that we were planning on going to recover the family skeleton-in-the-woods. She would have freaked. I was close enough to freaking myself.

It took my best stuff, my most subtle wheedling to get Mom to describe the location of her final confrontation with Whatshisname. I faked an academic interest, wanting to know why she thought no one had found him for so long. She said that it was because there is an unmarked side trail that goes to a lookout. She remembered going too far and Himself dragging her back to the right of an old oak tree, the kind of tree with huge limbs like arms splayed in every direction, great for climbing but spooky in dim light. From there it was just a few minutes to the spot, she thought, but she was not sure if everything took way longer than it seemed or the opposite. Time flew or dragged, one minute to the next.

There's no way I would have gone if Amy hadn't been so definite about it. I'm not blaming her or trying to say that I didn't know what I was getting into, because NONE of us knew what we were getting into, but before I went I had a twisted rope feeling in the pit of my gut and the closer we got to actually going, the worse I felt.

Creeped out, nauseated, and about to begin a search for the bones of the man who was not only my father but who had tried to murder both me and my mom, I felt like I should share my good fortune with my friends. Amy was already on board, it being her fault, I mean idea, that we were going in the first place. Whatshisname chose a spot that was not remote in the context of how remote things can be in this big country, but it was well off the beaten track for city types like us.

No public transport.

We needed a driver.

Carter was the lucky prize-winner. He was available, could get his hands on his parents' SUV and he was always making jokes about how he had a good sense of direction because his dad is Anishinaabe from a Mississauga band east of Toronto. I figured if he was pissed off when he found out that we weren't just going on a hike, I'd throw it back at him, and say we needed his woods lore.

Besides, Rich was out. Granny thought Rich was *beau* - cute. And that was with a head full of half-formed pseudo-dreads. He and Émilie were going shopping today.

I told Mom that I'd be going to a friend's place to watch a late-night pay-per-view ultimate fight and I'd be gone until the next day. If she ever figured out what we were doing, I was going to bring up the fact that I can't stand ultimate fighting and she should know that. None of this, then, could be my fault.

I didn't let her see my preparations - she was at work. Again. She'd have known in a millisecond what I was up to. I took gloves, a trowel, and a plastic-lined athletic bag for the dirty work. We had backpacks with food and water, a map of sorts that I had been able to download, and some vague references from Mom, as specific as I could get from her without setting off her alarms.

We took off at a civilized hour, heading south.

It was a broad-shouldered, plaid shorts-wearing October Saturday morning.

"You're giving me gas money, right?" Carter said when he realized how far we were going to drive. "I don't think anyone will notice the odometer, but they'll notice the gas. Why couldn't we go somewhere closer?"

"Yeah, no sweat," I replied, ignoring his second question. Our speed had decreased substantially, as we were now on a narrow, winding access road. Light reflecting from a lake to our left demanded our attention as rocky outcroppings and trees dominated the right. There was, on one side of the road or the other, the very occasional modest home and yard. With pickup trucks. Always pickup trucks.

Amy rode shotgun. She looked carefully at the directions I had scribbled. We were looking for a specific crossroad that would in one direction lead off to a private campground and the other to a path that linked up with the Rideau Trail, a system of walking routes that stretches from Ottawa to Kingston.

Carter turned into the campground and we parked near the office under a bright red maple tree. Amy got out to talk to the man who came from inside. I caught a glimpse of a balding middle-aged guy with a beer belly bursting out of a plaid shirt. I heard the last part of the conversation as I opened my door.

"...on a hike. We'd be happy to pay if you'd let us park here."

"Not necessary - just come in and buy something to drink when you get back - and be sure to lock your doors."

"Are you sure? We're city people - we're used to paying for parking." I saw the smile, the one that could get people to do things just by being, the smile that could seal a deal that had never been spoken. Amy's particular magic is subtle and powerful, a wordless enchantment that gets people to do her a favour and then makes them feel like she'd just done them one instead.

"Parking's free," the guy smiled.

I shouldered my small backpack and took the athletic bag in my right hand.

"What's that for?" Carter asked.

"It's the Bag of Undetermined Purpose," I replied as I walked briskly toward the trailhead.

"So is it a surprise or a mystery?" he said to Amy.

"Both," she said.

"Great," he sang sarcastically.

"It's better than being the Bag of Ill-Considered Futility! Or the Bag of Incomprehensible Folly!" She yanked the bag from my hand and ran ahead.

"That's not saying much!" Carter shouted. He looked at me narrowly. "What are you guys up to?"

"Just going on a hike in a place with a little family history."

"Yours or mine? This is probably unceded Algonquin territory, you know."

"All the more reason we need to do what we're going to do." Then I raced to catch up with Amy, leaving Carter with no option but to run as well, decreasing the risk step by step that he'd discover what we were actually doing there and then refuse to continue.

The walk was a deep breath, a long silent stretch, a dreamless sleep. The hardwood forest was approaching its annual peak of colour. Fierce red leaves in the maples, and poplars and birch trees were turning as well. The ground was soft, the air warm and dry, the trails were well marked and we were alone.

I was in the lead as I was supposed to be the one who sort of knew where we were going. Amy and Carter talked happily behind me.

"*Dagwaagin*." He pronounced the first syllable to sound like dug. "It's Anishnaabemowin for autumn."

"Cool," said Amy. "How much do you know - of Anishna ..."

"Anishnaabemowin. I can understand a little of what my dad says to me, but right now I can't say very much. Like any other language, you need to be surrounded by it to be able to have a conversation. I can probably say more than Chase can of *his* ancestral language."

"My mother's ancestral language is French. And autumn in French is ..."

"*L'automne*, loser," Carter smirked before I had a chance to remember.

I knew that. I couldn't help it if I was distracted, could I? I was saved from further abuse by the appearance of the spooky oak tree, the only reliable reference I had to the presence of the side trail I was looking for.

"This is the way," I said as I pointed off to the right.

"Really? We're going off the main trail? Is this why you made me come - to keep you guys safe from nature, like Indigenous people have been doing for European invaders for centuries?"

"Yup," Amy replied. "Wait a minute - that's a good question. What do we do if we meet a bear?"

"Easy," Carter said. "We run faster than Chase."

"That's all you have? That's your woods lore?" I objected over Amy's laughter.

"Don't need woods lore. Just need speed."

They continued to make fun of me behind my back while I slowed our pace and scanned for another side trail that was supposed to lead to an unmarked viewpoint. After a kilometre or so, I spotted a blue triangle pointing to the left and a small wooden sign that read View. I guess it wasn't unmarked anymore. The trail started to climb, snaking its way on a couple of gentle switchbacks, the terrain rockier than it had been.

I tried to picture Mom with me riding on her back being forced up this trail in the dark. Listening to Whatshisname's obsessive rantings. Telling her how much he loved us. Blaming her for not understanding, for calling the cops, for taking me away.

She must have been wild. Shivering in sweat. Thin, shackled breaths, restlessly quaking hands. Desperately visualizing resistance. Screaming. Running.

I stopped to put one hand on a tree, the rough bark a comforting familiarity. I look down at my own feet, reconnected with the present and kept walking.

As we arrived at the top of a ridge, we got the promised view. It wasn't postcard panoramic, but it was nature art, bold, bright, unique. I peered over the opposite side and tried to imagine the climax of that night, the final determined push, a slow-motion shot of a fully grown loser of a man tumbling down the steep slope.

He had to have travelled down a good distance, or someone would have found him a long time ago. There needed to be a reason no one had, and that reason must have had something to do with cover - trees, bushes, rocks, something that could hide a body from view. I decided on a couple of likely places to search and, putting my backpack down, I took the athletic bag from Amy and began a careful descent.

"What ARE you doing?" Carter shouted at me.

"You can tell him, if you dare," I shouted back. I didn't hear her response, if she made one, and I lost sight of them fairly quickly as I descended among the rocks. Grabbing hold of whatever limbs, branches, and roots that I could, I lowered myself, thinking about nothing but the phrase *three points of contact*. I don't like climbing, mostly because I don't like falling.

My muscles twitching with relief at the bottom, I opened the bag and took out the work gloves. Then, I held my breath and parted the stiff branches of a spiky shrub. Peering inside I cleared leaves aside, hoping against hope to see ... I wasn't sure what. Maybe some clothes that would cover the ghoulish remains, maybe a shoulder bone, or an arm. I didn't want to see a skull staring up at me with a gaping Halloween smile.

And I didn't.

I was relieved and disappointed to find nothing at all. But then I had to do it all over again. Find another likely spot, clear away brush, peer inside, and poke around for remains. My legs began to cramp and I had to stop and stretch them out. The emotional weight of what I was doing, the sheer absurdity of the situation made me get weird. I began to call out.

"Da-aave …. Where are you, you psycho wannabe killer?" I sang softly from between clenched teeth as I searched the leafy surfaces under branches and the dark crevasses between rocks. Because I never used Whatshisname's given name, it helped me achieve a little distance, even if it was creepy and surreal.

"Oh, Daaaa-aaaave!" I looked above me and tried to picture him falling, rolling, bouncing, a person no more, just a body. I worked myself to a sitting position, bracing for a forward reach under the prickly branch of a fir tree that had rooted in the rock of the slope. My right hand reached out and I raised the branch just enough to take a tentative peek.

"Who the hell is Dave?" asked a loud, deep voice coming from the base of the tree.

"Shit!" I shouted as I jumped backward. "What are you doing there?"

"Same as you, I thought," Carter said. "Amy said we're looking for bones. Call me impatient, but you're taking forever, so I thought I'd help. By the way, do you realize what sort of bad juju this is?"

"Juju? Seriously?"

"Hey, in any language, in any culture, messing with the bones of your ancestors is asking for trouble."

"I've already got lots of trouble - this is supposed to help avoid any more."

"Yeah, Amy filled me in. You could have just told me, you know. It's not like I wouldn't have come."

"I was just trying to give you an out. In case this backfires, you can say you didn't know."

"Fair enough. Did you look under this garbage bag over here?"

"What garbage bag?"

"This one," said Amy. I guess both she and Carter had found a better, easier way down the slope and had come up from below. From their vantage point they could see quite a bit that was obscured from above.

"There shouldn't be a bag covering anything. Unless …."

"Unless maybe Gary did it to mark the spot for himself," said a low gravelly voice from my right side.

And the man it was coming from carried a shotgun.

# Chapter Twenty-Three

## Long Time No See

"I guess I owe you a debt of gratitude," he said through a 1978 Camaro moustache that outlined the top of his narrow mouth. "I would have found that, but it would have taken some time."

"Who are you?" Amy asked, the first of us to find a voice.

"None of your business." He swung the shotgun up to his shoulder, to rest pointing behind him. He was fairly tall and thin, with black and grey hair and a hooded green coat that came to about mid-thigh. "Now YOU," he said in my direction, "I bet you're the snot-nosed dipshit kid Gary talked about."

I must have reacted, maybe started backwards.

"Don't worry, don't worry, this thing isn't even loaded." He pulled the shotgun off his shoulder and broke it open. "See?" He made a show of the empty barrel, then dug into his jacket pocket, pulled out a shell and put it in, snapping the weapon shut, all the while maintaining eye contact with me. "But I guess it's loaded now, so if you're experiencing some discomfort, I would understand. Not that I mean to frighten you all, but, see, from my point of view you've probably already murdered once. Now, Gary, you killed him with a peanut. It would take a little more to put me in the ground."

"What do you want?" I asked, as casually as I could.

He laughed. "Notice how you didn't deny it. It's funny how a shotgun affects a conversation." He took his eyes off me and looked down. "I am assuming," he said, pointing to the athletic bag on the ground beside me, "*that* is how you intend to transport the remains out of here. That'll come in handy." He looked at Amy. "Now - you, sweetheart - have a look and tell us what's under that garbage bag."

"Wait! Let me!" I said, taking a step forward. Carter moved as well.

"Stop right there," he said as he pointed the gun - first at me and then at Carter. "I said I wanted *her* to look. Do you get me? And you," he said loudly, glaring at Carter, "my aboriginal friend, you keep your distance as well."

"Indigenous," Carter pronounced coldly. "And we're not friends."

"Chase, that's fine. I can do it," Amy said.

"That's right - that's the name! Chase! Gary couldn't stand you. Lucky for you that you got him first. Now, let's have a look."

I threw Amy the work gloves and she put them on while walking slowly over to the half-buried garbage bag. She bent over to give it a tug and found that the edges had been weighted down with stones. She removed about half of them along two edges and peeled the bag back.

It took a moment for my brain to catch up to my eyes, to register what was in front of us. A jumble of human remains along with traces of partially decayed clothing. Some of the bones were in a pile, one body part indistinguishable from another, but it looked as if much of it was covered with earth, the result of many years of lying there, the seasons doing their bit along with the decomposers to make the body part of the landscape.

"How about that? You learn something new every day, they say. Today, I get to see what a real live dead person looks like after fifteen years. And I learn that Gary was not as big a bullshitter as I thought."

"Did he do this - make the pile? Cover it up?" I asked.

"I suppose he did. He mentioned something about coming without a bag, the dumb shit. He thought he'd be returning, of course." I didn't see any bag with this guy, either, so what sort of dumber shit did that make him? He put the shotgun under one arm, stretched the other one out and sat down on a rock.

"Now, you'll be finishing what you started, sweetheart. I want everything in that bag you brought. Do it now."

"Let me do it - he was my father."

"That's right. A piece of work, too, from what I heard. Until your mother caved his skull in."

What?

"Sure, go ahead and have some quality father-son time, just hurry the fuck up. You two help him."

I took three or four steps to where Amy stood and took the gloves from her. I squatted and opened up the athletic bag wide. Holding my breath, I carefully picked up the bigger pieces and gingerly placed them in the bag. I tried to be methodical, attempting to distance myself from the fact of who this was. Having a stranger with a shotgun standing nearby probably helped me as I picked, pulled, sorted and then dug as much as I could. There wasn't anything like a full skeleton there. Maybe scavenging wildlife had taken some away, or maybe Gary had moved some and not marked it.

Both Amy and Carter came to help, using the many available leaves and the old plastic bag to avoid touching the remains with their bare hands.

I did okay. I only puked twice.

The first time was when I found the skull. It was partially bashed in on one side, kind of above the left eye socket. I was weirdly embarrassed, even ashamed of it so I put it in the bag as soon as I could. Then I puked. The second time was when he insisted that I take the feet out of the shoes. I think he thought it was funny. Both times I crawled away and heaved under a tree.

The whole time, the guy kept talking. "Besides being a liar, Gary's biggest problem was that he was such a lazy shit. Probably couldn't make himself dig up these bones properly. Didn't want to get his hands dirty. And he was too comfortable by half. I think I met the reason why the other night, yessir - a good-lookin' woman. No wonder he wanted to hang around, see how far his charms would take him. I might try myself. Maybe you'll put in a good word for me."

Trying not to gag as I finished the gruesome excavation, I was also nurturing a growing sense of all-consuming hatred for this guy. There was only one reason he wanted the bag of remains, and that had to be to blackmail Mom into ... doing who knows what. I had another Gary on my hands, maybe a worse kind of Gary, and I had to handle this one carefully. My anger helped me focus, settling my stomach and turning my mind to finding a way of changing my situation. I made the briefest of eye contact with Amy and I chose to see approval - we had to do something.

If he didn't have the shotgun, he wouldn't have any advantage over the three of us - we could take him or, I was sure, at least outrun him, given our youthful vigour and his crapulent salt-and-pepper skinniness. I wondered if I could get an advantage, one not shotgun-related, and maybe throw him off his game. I finished our excavation, zipped up the bag and picked it up. Then, I remembered the conversation Mom had had with the Great Detective and his sidekick. I took a chance.

"Here you go ... Mike." He looked right at me. Gotcha.

I held the bag out for him to take - it was heavier than I thought it would be, and my outstretched arm descended a little as I stood there staring at him.

"Just put it down and back away," he said.

I set the bag on a flat rock and waited for him to reach for it.

"Thank you *all* so much for your help," he said as he came forward, left hand out to take the bag, right hand holding the shotgun. One way or another, this was my only opportunity to go for the gun, when he couldn't hold it with both hands. I got ready to spring.

I never got the chance.

Carter was faster. In two quick bounds he had both hands on the shotgun. His left hand pushed the butt down and his right twisted the barrel up. He straightened his legs and used his back and shoulders to rip the gun from the older man's hand, took three quick steps and turned around, levelling the weapon at our opponent.

It took a few seconds for all of us to realize the power shift that had just happened.

"Nice!" was all I could think of to say.

"Now hold on. That thing isn't a toy, chief." He dropped the bag and I scrambled ahead to pick it up.

Carter's eyes narrowed as his shoulders dropped a little. "Really? Did I hear you right? Did you just call me CHIEF?"

"Okay, now ...."

"And you think I don't know how to use this thing?" Carter quickly pumped the shotgun, brought it to his shoulder, aimed it at the older man, and, while Amy and I were transfixed in shock, he pointed the weapon and pulled the trigger.

# Chapter Twenty-Four

## I Hate It When People Make Puns with My Name

I jumped and squeezed my eyes shut.

Amy went, "Eep!"

Birds squawked and cheeped and flapped away. Forest creatures scurried for cover as the crash of the shotgun seemed to linger in the dry air. When our antagonist looked up I was pretty sure his hair was greyer.

"That's what I think of you, asshole, and this is what I think of your toy gun!" Carter took a step forward and launched the shotgun into the air with all his strength. It landed out of sight with something between a splash and a thud. Amy and I looked at each other and then at Carter.

"Now - you can go look for it if you like," he said. And then to us, he added with a smile, "Okay, let's go!" and bolted. We knew leadership when we saw it and took off after him, leaving Mike, and I was pretty sure that's who he was, collecting himself at the bottom of the ridge.

The trip up was easier than the way down had been except for the new physical and psychological load of Whatshisname's remains. I don't think it was the exertion that made my legs feel wobbly and my whole body feel pukey. The confrontation with Mike hadn't helped. I staggered ahead as fast as I could, slowing the others down. We got a couple of hundred metres away and slowed down a bit. I took the opportunity to put my arms through the handles of the athletic bag, trying to carry it more like a backpack.

"Carter, that was amazing!" Amy gasped as we stopped for a breather.

"Naah. He didn't want to shoot us. His vibe is more thief than murderer."

"Still," I panted, "you did it, and it was. Amazing. I kinda wish we still had the shotgun, though."

"I suppose, but I wanted to give him a reason to go in another direction. Those things are expensive."

"Why ... Why did you call him Mike?" Amy asked between breaths.

"I think I know who he is. He was meeting with my mom the night Big Don died."

"HE'S her alibi? That's awful!"

"Yeah, and I don't think it was a date. He's probably just picking up the blackmail where Gary left it, and today he was doing what we're doing - getting the goods before the bad weather sets in."

A shout and the boom of a shotgun blast broke up our meeting.

"I think he might have changed his mind about the murdery stuff," I said as I pushed them ahead of me on the trail and we renewed our run.

He was pretty fast for an old fart. I couldn't believe he'd been in training or anything, as con artists and blackmailers don't usually do a lot of wind sprints, so he must have had some innate ability. To be fair, though, aspiring animators don't interval train either, so maybe my youthful vigour was inadequate. And the bouncing, awkward weight of Whatshisname's bones was taking the spring out of my step.

We were running down a section of trail wider than most because it was part of an old railway bed. As we approached the turn we needed to take, there was another concussive boom behind us. Mike was getting closer and he was letting us know he still meant business.

"Guys, wait!" I panted. Both Amy and Carter were ahead of me and had to come back. We only had about a minute before Mike would catch up. "You go ahead - you're faster without me. I'll lead him off in another direction. If I can I'll call or text, but if I can't, I'll meet you back at the car, in like an hour."

"He's not gonna shoot us," Carter maintained. "He's only trying to scare us."

"Well, it's working!" I took off down the old railbed. I was pretty sure that Mikey saw which way I was heading, which suited my purposes.

Sweaty, scared, and increasingly sore, I turned at the first opportunity to get off the main trail. The problem was that I was now heading in the opposite direction of my friends, away from help or escape. And I had an ever-growing awareness that I seemed to be in some kind of bad movie. Chasing Chase was the working title. I would have to change that. If it was going to have a crowd-pleasing but sell-out ridiculous ending, the one where I actually survive, a talking lion or friendly wizard would have to find a way to help me out.

Inevitably, one of my tired feet didn't get lifted high enough as I shuffled through the forest. Instead of swinging ahead to propel me on my next step, it ran smack into a tree root and I fell forward onto my hands and knees. Another bad movie cliché, but if nothing changed, I was in danger of providing the non-existent viewer with something rather different - an uncompromised *good* ending. A cinéma-vérité finish. Before I die, there would be all manner of hand-held camera angles, leafy footfalls, and heart-pounding huffing and puffing. My shocking violent death would impress the critics.

I heard running sounds behind me and I thought Mike was catching up. Despite his working-man appearance, maybe Mike was into quality cinema. He'd want to give the critics that depressing finish they craved. I was out of steam, so I did the only thing I could. I unslung the bag of bones from my back and put it in the middle of the trail where Mike would easily find it. I limped off in the direction opposite to the one he'd be coming from. I scrambled up the back of one of those big boulders some lazy glacier left behind thousands of years ago and I waited, keeping an eye on things. I wanted to watch him take it, watch to make sure he would no longer be on my tail. It was my way of ensuring that I lived to fight the good fight another day. I'd taken care of Gary, or Mom had, and maybe she'd even taken care of Don, so we could probably handle Mike if we worked together.

But Mike never showed. I waited and waited. I crept back to the bag and picked it up. No Mike. I walked back to the trail in the old railbed. No Mike. I climbed to a high point a couple of hundred metres away to try phoning Amy and Carter but the reception was crap. And when I came down, no Mike.

Had he got tired and gone home? Did he run out of shotgun ammo? Did he step aside for a smoke? Why would he bother running after us, shooting up the forest, just to go home when he was close to winning?

That had to be it, I thought as I found the right trail back to the campground, turning at a weathered signpost. He didn't know he was about to win, he didn't realize that I was giving up. He ran out of gas. I had just about convinced myself of that when I crossed the access road that had first brought us here several hours before. Switching the bones bag from one hand to the other, I walked up the road waving at Carter and Amy as I saw them leaning against Carter's SUV with drinks in their hands. I gratefully accepted one from Carter and took four huge gulps from it as Amy took the bag from me. I sat down on a low concrete curb with my legs splayed and smiled up at my friends.

"We did it!" I said.

"Yeah," said Carter.

"About that ...," Amy began.

Shit.

"Okay, what about that - what happened?"

"This guy Mike is maybe smarter than we thought," Carter said.

"It took him a while, but he figured out that he didn't have to chase us." Amy gave the bag a soft tap with the toe of her shoe.

"Why not? Come on! I have the bones. Whatshisname ... in the bag, so to speak." They were snatching defeat from the jaws of victory and they needed to tell me why.

Amy sat beside me on the curb. "He found us here a half hour ago. He said that you'll give him that bag, and if you don't, he won't alibi your mom for the night Don fell in front of the train. Sorry."

"He has to! If Mom's in jail, she can't help him bilk orphans out of their inheritance."

"If he doesn't have that bag, he doesn't have any power over your mom," Amy said. "So maybe he wouldn't get rich, but he'd enjoy seeing her go on trial."

"That's what he said. And it sounded like he meant it." Carter kicked a stone across the gravel parking lot. "Did you really kill Gary with a peanut?"

"Yeah," I said absent-mindedly. "Wait - no - Mom did, no ... never mind, forget I said that. I don't know anything anymore."

"He gave us his number," Amy said, standing, "and you're supposed to text him when we get back to town."

"Great," I sighed, putting my head between my knees. When I brought my head back up, I asked to be left alone for a few minutes. Amy and Carter got back into the car and I sat looking at the athletic bag, having a staring contest with Whatshisname inside. I could hold a stare as long as his bashed-in eyeless skull, but I couldn't compete with that toothy smile.

# Chapter Twenty-Five

## Some Skeletons Should Stay Closeted. Others Not.

You know, I was glad to give Mike the bones after all. Think of all the trouble I avoided. I didn't have to hide them from Mom, who would have had a full-body freak if she found them. That means I didn't have to sneak out in the middle of the night and bury them like a serial perv, or cut a makeshift hidey-hole in the floor of my room, or grind them up for lawn fertilizer or any of the other things I had been considering.

But it did mean that I had to start planning. I had to keep track of Mike while maintaining a good arm's length between him and Mom. Until I figured out a satisfying conclusion to the story of Whatshisname's journey from forest to very well-hidden grave or dumpster, or wherever he ended up, I needed to be a shield between Mom and the world.

Because I am not stupid, Mike did not get his bag of bones until he gave his statement to the cops. Being who he is, it was hard to tell if the cops thought he had any credibility, but his statement was enough to maintain the status quo. Detectives Reynolds and Tremblay stayed away. I don't think it helped them that they had detained, and then been forced to let go, the woman that GareBear was living with. They were working on an understanding of the two deaths, tying them together through Mom. Maybe that didn't play very well with their bosses. It might have made them look a little desperate.

How did I know that? I didn't. But Amy's dad is a Crown prosecutor. And Amy asks him hypothetical questions about cases in other cities, pretending an interest in the justice system. She takes advantage of the thirst for meaningful conversation any regular parent of a normal teenager has, not asking about Gary or Don but about police procedure and thresholds of evidence and all that.

Amy is handy to have around. Indispensable. And she was still hanging around with me knowing Mom is a murderer. Okay, Amy didn't agree about all that, but still, here she is and here I am and whenever I was not thinking about murders and bones and psycho losers, I was thinking about Amy.

Her hair. Her mouth.

Her collar bones. I'm not kidding, who knew clavicles could be lethally sexy?

"Oh, man," I said, completely absent-minded.

"What is it?" asked Mom.

"Hmm? Nothing."

I was drying dishes. The cranky woman to the left of me was washing. The occasional meal and dishes routine was becoming one of the rare opportunities I had to speak with She-Who-Gave-Me-Life. She had increased her hours at work, given that we had a financial hole to fill since Big Don bit the dust. I had school, work, a social life, and a cover-up to complete, one that had to keep Mom in the dark and that also had to effectively deal with Shotgun Mikey.

"That was a big sigh for nothing."

"Dunno - guess I was just thinking about a few things."

Besides Amy's collar bones, I had been mulling a few other things over. I wanted to ask Mom about that night fifteen years ago when Whatshisname died, about the skull-bashing part of the story that she hadn't shared with me. Had she done that? If she had - HOW had she done that? And why not tell me? If the rest of the story was true, and I thought it probably was, why not tell me that part?

I didn't know how to put that question without revealing our bone-collecting trip into the woods, so I just said, "Just thinking about a few things. You and your killing spree, for one."

"That's not funny." She didn't look at me but instead gave a pasta pot a particularly vigorous scrub.

"Sorry - I just figured joking was the best way to deal with it. The cops are so stupid if they think ... you know. I know this is none of my business (it SO was my business), and you've got it under control (not even close), but this Mike guy, the one who's maybe the only reason the cops don't think you killed that Don guy ..." I paused to look at her, test the waters.

"What about him?"

The waters were a little rough, but I could handle that.

"Is he giving you any other sort of ... trouble? Is he liable to get in the way of The Plan?"

"Not yet."

"But you're expecting a certain amount of interference?" I really wanted to say expecting the shit to hit the fan, but you know adults and their childishness about language.

"I'm not sure what to expect."

"Did he have anything to do with why you needed to make money?"

"You mean from Don."

"Yeah."

"Yes - I needed a quick five hundred dollars and Don promised it to me. All I had to do was front him rather more than that. It was a risk."

"And the five hundred - that was to pay Mike?"

"To get him off my back. I was supposed to get it all back from Don in a matter of days. He just needed time to, what did he say, liquidate some assets? I was desperate. Mike was blackmailing me like Gary did - threatening to reveal what Gary found."

"Have you heard from him lately? Does he still want the money?"

"I'm sure he does, but maybe the cops threw him off a bit. He may be laying low."

"I need to ask you something. Why do the remains - Whatshisname's bones - even matter? If the cops find them, it just proves he went for a walk, got lost and died of exposure, right?" This was the skull-bashing-in issue, just in not so many words.

"Maybe," she said defensively. "But maybe it makes them ask all sorts of questions, maybe conduct a lengthy and undoubtedly painful investigation. I don't want to go there; I left that part of my life behind a long time ago and I don't want anything to do with it."

That was a good lie. It was all true. But it avoided the real truth, that the bashed-in skull would lead to far more uncomfortable questions. She didn't want to tell me about it, I got that. Her attitude, her defensiveness told me that I'd done the right thing, though. When Mike got his bag of bones, there was one important element missing. When he discovered it, he'd be pissed, maybe violently so. But in the meantime, I'd have room to prepare, opportunity to be creative.

I just had to stay away from the guest room. From the box with Amazon packing tape, the one perched on a shelf in the closet. From the bubble-wrapped smiling bashed-in skull tucked inside.

# Chapter Twenty-Six
## It Is SO a Word.

*A normally quiet street. Squat apartment buildings. A community centre. A couple of schools. And seven stop signs in ten blocks.*

*Darkly tinted glass prevents eye contact with the shadowy figure inside the compact car. Mothers grab children's hands and retreat away from the curb. Cyclists wave him through the intersection, regardless of right of way. A crossing guard bravely stands her ground as brakes heat and bind, rubber grips road as the car's chassis lurches forward and then back on its suspension.*

*She ushers people between white lines, her only defense a tiny octagon, the red shield that said STOP. Her front foot not yet back on the curb, clouds of exhaust envelop the intersection.*

*The race to the next stop sign begins. It is a race of one, a race against neither opponent nor clock. It's a contest of perception, an inner struggle the driver has here and everywhere. There is no question. He must never EVER waste a moment of precious, irreplaceable, finite life, by going slower than he had to.*

*One more intersection. One more stop sign. One lone figure looking to cross, then moving slowly into the middle of the street. Sunglasses turn to face the oncoming vehicle. Shoulders square as feet are planted. He is the immovable object, his eyes searching the windshield for those of the driver. Brakes bind once more as the warm rubber grips the pavement and rolling wheels suddenly rest.*

*The driver looks into the sunglasses and sees the front of his car, sees its animalistic posture, poised as if to pounce and kill. And he sees himself and experiences doubt as he never has before. The question occurs to him, the one he never thought about before. And the answer is no longer so clear.*


"Gimme a break - half the people in the world drive like that. And it's still lame. You've got two now - a cyclist who thinks he owns the road and now a driver who stops too fast? These are not villains, these are not interesting antagonists. You might as well add in the jerk in the coffee shop. They're just urban wallpaper. Selfish and flawed like everyone else."

"But they are all alienated in their own way, even if it's just because they never learned to see themselves the way other people do."

"Sure, but who cares? You need someone we can get behind as a villain. And that means someone who enjoys villainy, or at least rationalizes it to the point that they think it's the right way to go."

"Maybe we take a different approach," I said as I checked out a few internet dictionaries. "If you want creepy, I can do creepy. This one's ready-made - *predaperv.*"

"Is it as gross as it sounds?"

"Pretty much - a guy who's out to do as many women as possible, the younger the better."

"And you're going to make him into a character in an animated feature?"

"Maybe not. Here's one you don't want to know about - *predapedo.* AND - never heard this before - *predapotamus.* A polka-dot-wearing office harpy. Loud, whining, dramatic, and self-destructive."

"That's not a word. And it's misogynistic."

"It's a word if it's ... a *word,*" I sighed. "But it's out. I guess I should give up on the *preda*-somethings or *para*-somethings, and the word *predacite* is just confusing."

Amy was the wall upon which my spitballs were landing. I know that's gross, but it's a gross metaphor to begin with. She was using most of her brain to work on her Hamlet essay. I hadn't really got to mine yet, as I was avoiding the inevitable slide into anger and frustration associated with the Dreary Dane. However, I would have been happy to have been the wall upon which her literary spitballs stuck. I might have liked it, even in a disturbingly literal way, but she didn't need me to do that for her.

I tried not to think about all the things that Amy did not need me for. Forget BOB, there was an unending stream of guys who wanted to take her places, buy her things, and get close to her everything. I had never known her to let anyone pay for her, she never accepted gifts (she called them bribes), and I never asked her about the other stuff.

I had always thought that a good visual imagination and an innate storytelling ability were strengths. It turned out they were also a good way to torment myself. Gary had shown me that as I imagined him trying to get it on with my mother. Amy was another case. I saw her frequently in my mind's eye, in the soft focus of a widescreen Amy aura, looking me in the eye and smiling that smile. I got butterflies when I hit the image just right, but they turned into very jealous bugs if I let my mind consider the reality that she was spending time with perfect-smile fashion-footwear BOB, smiling, probably making out.

Two kinds of torment there. I know which one I prefer, but torment is torment.

"Maybe you should just focus on learning how to draw." I must have been staring at her without realizing it and when I came back to myself, she was looking at me as if I were a puzzle she had to solve. "Maybe the ideas need to come out of your fingers rather than out of your head."

"I need an idea first."

"Why?

"Because I DO."

"Maybe you don't, though. Maybe drawing will help generate the idea, you know, organically."

"What do I start with, though?"

"Easy - a self-portrait."

Great.

There were about a hundred things wrong with that idea, starting with the fact that I am about the least interesting subject I can think of.

Drawing me would be an exercise in dull, a lab in tiresome, an entire course of pointless.

And how am I supposed to know what I really look like?

# Chapter Twenty-Seven

## It Is Not My Pleasure to Serve You

It took a few days for Mike to make his inevitable discovery and call me up for a chat.

"Did you think I wouldn't notice?"

"You've got what you need."

"There might be a world of information in what you didn't give me. So unless you do, our deal's off, boy."

"What're you gonna do now, Mikey? Go to the cops and say you were lying? You made it up? You know they already checked. You know that we don't need you anymore."

"First, I'll give 'em the real deal - that your sweet-assed mommy was gone *before* eight o'clock. Then, I'll give 'em the bones I have, you little dipshit. See where that takes 'em."

"Hey, it's better than having to put up with YOU for the rest of our lives. And I'd like to be there when you turn up with a bag of bones you just happened to find somewhere. Gee, Mikey, just how is it that you know who the dead guy is and that you have his bones? Could it be that you killed him all those years ago? Knock yourself out."

And I hung up.

Well, this sucked. Mom had left the bar *before* eight? It was only a few minutes' walk to Rideau Station. Detective Sergeant Reynolds and his moustache would start with her again, and the new timeline might be the thin edge of the wedge that they could use to accuse her of Gary's murder as well. The cops would be so much happier if the murders could be connected. Ottawa's own Black Widow. They could write books and make big consultant fees on the Netflix Original movie. I couldn't give Mike the opportunity to tell them. I had to edit him out, delete him from the story.

But how?

A major distraction entered into my life just as I set my mind to the task of creating a solution to the Mikey issue. I got a promotion.

I guess my semi-half-assed work ethic was better than some. I showed up for all my shifts on time. I sorta did what I thought they wanted me to. Carry this, stack that. And my manager, Gene whose-surname-I-never-learned, thought I could handle the Customer Service desk two shifts a week.

OhmyGOD. Customer Disservice is SUCH a pain in the ass. People expect you to know everything, be able to solve their tiniest problems, exchange crappy used things for brand new, give refunds like they are Christmas presents, know and care about all the rip-off lottery tickets they can buy, and then be patient as the line gets longer and longer as they take more and more time in deciding which particular way they will lose their pension cheques this month. My only advantage was that I was not yet nineteen and therefore not legally allowed to sell tobacco products. I needed backup.

Arjun was it. He was probably the friendliest person at the store - maybe thirty-five, a cheesy moustache, male pattern baldness and a growing paunch. It didn't matter how cranky customers were, Arjun always had a smile, and seemed to figure out a solution. He had a wife and a kid and another on the way. And he never complained about how hard he had to work.

I could never be an Arjun. Forget the married-with-kid thing, which I refuse to even think about, but friendly and smiling? All the time?

"It's not difficult, Chase," he said to me in his gentle South Asian accent. "If you smile at people and speak to them warmly, they most often will reciprocate." As I looked at him, my doubt must have been clear on my face, because he continued. "And when you have done all you can do and they are still not happy, you let them go and be unhappy. Never carry their unhappiness for them."

I thought Arjun should have his own afternoon TV show. And, when I thought about it, he might even have a novel approach to parasites and predators. Let them swim in their own crapulence. It was an interesting philosophical point, too, one that I may have had time for another day. That day, though, my "training" was getting in the way of my Amy time. She was fitting me in instead of hanging out with BOB and was supposed to text me. We were going to hang out, connect, converse, do whatever until she inevitably fell for me and tried to have her way with me in some safe, private and completely spontaneous context.

Yeah, that's me long-terming again, my reality gap. I still hadn't managed a summer holiday hug or a mistletoe Christmas kiss.

Then some lady wanted to return apple juice she bought last week because it was on sale THIS week. So, I tried Arjun's soft approach. I was okay for the first minute. I can't help it if I get annoyed with stupid people. I kept telling her I could only refund her the sale price, because we're not a furniture store with a thirty-day price guarantee.

"But it's cheaper now," she said, looking at me over her glasses.

"Yes, but we don't refund price differences."

"But I paid too much."

"No, you didn't - it wasn't on sale last week."

"It is NOW. That's why I want my money back."

It went on like that for a while. I said she was being unreasonable. She called me rude. I'm sure she thought that I was just a know-nothing snot-nosed post-pubescent loser. I *know* she was a brain-dead ill-tempered blue-haired harpy. And I was just about to tell her so when Arjun came over to bail me out.

Then, when I stepped back, relinquishing my position at the firing line to He-Who-Is-Temperamentally-Suited-to-Arguing-With-Old-Ladies, I got the message.

It was from Amy. I thought.


**Amy**: You've got something I want.
**Me**: OK.

**Amy**: You know what I mean?
**Me**: I hope I do.

That should have given it away. Amy does NOT flirt with me. Not in person and definitely not on her phone.

**Amy**: You want your pretty little girlfriend back?
**Me**: ?
**Amy**: Bring the smiling head. Dipshit.

That sounded like Mikey. OHMYGOD I'd been close to sexting with Mikey.

*Puke*!

Worse, he had Amy's phone. And Amy went wherever her phone went.

**Me**: What do you want?
**Amy's Phone**: You know. Bring it.
**Me**: When and where?
**Amy's Phone**: Tunney's Pasture 7:30. Wait for instructions.
**Me**: OK.
**Amy's Phone**: Don't fuck with me
**Me**: Send me a picture of Amy.
**Amy's Phone**: Fuck you. Don't be late.

"Arjun, I gotta go! Emergency!" I blurted in his direction as I vaulted over the Customer Service desk and ran out the door. My bike was chained up outside and I frantically unlocked it, jumped on and took off for home. It was just past six o'clock and if I made time I could be there in fifteen minutes, grab Whatshisname in his box and then jump on a passing number 51 to get to the LRT station at Tunney's.

I pumped like crazy, dodging cars and jumping curbs, trying not to be a bike-borne predator but at the same time figuring routes and making plans. All of that was more painfully difficult because of the engrossing, sickening fear in the pit of my stomach, the dread of what that skinny asshole-that-walks-like-a-man might have done to Amy and how it was all my fault.

# Chapter Twenty-Eight
## I Learn to Speak Douchebag

My phone was in my right hand. Whatshisname's box was perched on my hip and secured under the crook of my left elbow. It was 7:23 and I stood on a brightly lit platform at Tunney's Pasture, still wearing the black golf shirt that was an excuse for a uniform at the Grocery Barn. I used the short cotton sleeves to mop my forehead, sweaty despite the chill of an October evening, as I looked around, trying to get a glimpse of Mike or Amy.

At 8:03, the phone dinged a message.

> **Amy's Phone**: Dipshit
> **Me**: Y
> **Amy's Phone**: Put it on the rear seat of the second car going downtown. Next train.
> **Me**: Leave it?
> **Amy's Phone**: Leave it
> **Me**: Where's Amy?
> **Amy's Phone**: You'll find out. Same place. Next train coming. You better hurry.

Mikey wanted to pretend he was a sophisticated spy with a sneaky drop routine. I stuffed the phone in my pocket as the next train approached. I watched and waited, anticipating each stage of the LRT dance.

Train stops.

Doors open.

Passengers exit.

Passengers enter, pause to scan the options, and flop on best available seats.

But Mikey's instructions were lousy. Technically, each train had only two cars, but each car had two sections - one with space for a driver and one without. Did the asshat know that?

I did the simplest thing I could - went to the end of the train, put the box on an empty seat and jumped out the door. My timing was off, though.

"Excuse me? Did you leave this behind?" A middle-aged guy in an Ottawa Redblacks hat held out the Amazon box.

Shit! Why do people have to be so helpful?

"Um, no ... but ... yes, I did, but ...."

I stood there for the briefest moment, wanting to tell him that the cube he was holding contained my father's smiling skull. Then I pretended to be grateful, grumbling a stammered thank you and took the box. As the guy boarded the train and the doors closed, I frantically dug out my phone and swiped to get into the messaging app.

> **Me**: Problem! Passenger gave it back to me. I have to wait until the next train!
>
> **Amy's Phone**: I told you not to fuck with me.
>
> **Me**: I'm not - and which second car - the very last seat at the very back?
>
> **Amy's Phone**: What else?
>
> **Me**: OK - the very very back.
>
> **Amy's Phone**: Last chance, dipshit.

I'm the dipshit? Compared to him?

And whatever the hell is a dipshit, anyway? It must be douchebag for something bad.

Very few things make me angry like being called stupid by someone who is very clearly a micro-brained knuckle-dragging slack-jawed product of a long-drained gene pool. What made it ever so much worse was that he was getting the better of me. I was being forced to do what he wanted because he had leverage over me, because he was freer than I was, him being a wide-ranging immoral lowlife piece of shit.

Seething, I boarded the train, went to the rear and left the box on a seat. Other passengers stayed away from me, maybe sensing my rage, and this time I waited until right before the doors closed before leaping out. I watched Whatshisname on his own seat slowly pulling away, feeling powerless now that I had nothing. No bones, no skull and no Amy.

I looked up at the LRT route map and saw that the next station along, Bayview, was where he must be, a station where he could continue going east or transfer to the north-south Trillium line, or just take off on foot or in a car and I would never be able to follow. I waited for the next westbound train and jumped on, half-running its entire length before realizing Amy was not on it. Then I realized that she might not be - that Mike never said she would be, only that I would find out where she was.

And then ... what if she was on the next train and not this one? Or worse, what if he left me something to find on the next train, and not this one? I hadn't been able to properly search this one and the doors were closing. I flipped a mental coin and jumped out, thinking that the next one made more sense anyway, given the period of time that it would have taken for Whatshisname in his box to reach Bayview Station.

Four minutes. The next train was in four minutes. I paced up and down the platform, using every profane word in my vocabulary and making up a few new ones. I still haven't figured out what an ass-sac is, but I was happy with it then. I saw the train approaching and positioned myself to get on the front and work my way through all of the cars as fast as I could.

My hands must have been shaking and I don't know what my face must have looked like, but a few passengers threw startled, wary, maybe even concerned glances in my direction. I ignored them all as I darted through the doors and fiercely scanned the cars for anything that Mike might have left for me to find. Fighting butterflies, nausea, and B.O. so bad even I noticed it, I got to the last car and saw it - a small box with the word

DIPSHIT scrawled on it. I picked it up just before the doors closed and leaped out as the train started to move. I sat down on a bench and ripped the box open. There was an old torn envelope inside with an address written on it - 179 Finch.

And below the envelope, Amy's phone. It gave me the creeps, like I was looking at some part of her that Mikey had held in his pervy palms. I stuffed it in my back pocket and dug out my own phone to find out just where the hell 179 Finch was. I hadn't realized I was holding my breath until I saw that Finch Avenue was fairly close. Letting my breath go, I got to my feet and charged out of the station.

I hadn't noticed the wind on the way to the station, but I did now - it was frigid, my sweat-soaked shirt suddenly making me shiver as I bounded across Holland Avenue and down the paved recreational pathway. There were no cyclists, and no other pedestrians as I loped parallel to Scott Street for what can only be a few hundred metres.

But I was getting tired. A long day - crazy geezers at work, frantic predatory cycling, learning to speak douchebag. I was reaching the end of my rope, which wasn't very long to begin with. I pulled out Amy's phone and entered her passcode. Yes, I looked over her shoulder, and yes, I know it's creepy. But in times like this, that sort of thing can come in handy.

I looked at her messages to see if anyone else had tried to contact her, to see if anyone else was missing her. There were a couple of messages from BOB. He was looking for her and sounded annoyed that she was not at his beck and call this evening. I deleted them. They'd just piss Amy off.

If I was near the end of my rope, Amy must be ... well, we'd heard a lot about PTSD the last while and I had to hope she wouldn't develop it. I hung in there, trying to tell my aching feet, stinging lungs and shaky legs to just get on with it.

There, on the corner I saw the blue street sign - Finch - and veered left. It's mostly a residential area, some brand-new condominiums and otherwise small frame and stucco houses very near to the street on narrow lots. I searched them for numbers, quickly finding 175 and 183 with nothing but a crater in the middle, a huge hole in the ground surrounded by temporary steel fencing. A sign demanding hard hats and steel-toed boots hung on it, and just beside it, a much smaller hand-drawn 179.

There was nothing there. I stopped in front of the fence and paced back and forth trying to figure out where Amy might be. But the only impression I got was the smell - dusty, woody, stale and obsolete, the smell of age and abandonment.

Frustration squeezing out of my pores, fear and cold making my sweaty hair stand on end, I could think of nothing to do but shout, "AMY!"

And again, "AMY!"

I heard something. I stood still, not breathing

And it was there. A voice. A dull thumping and a rattle.

Snaking to the right of the fence was a driveway - more of a track - that led to a wooden shed, shadowed from the streetlights, at the far end of the lot.

"Amy? Tell me you're in there. Amy?"

"... in here! I've been shouting for DAYS!" I heard as I approached the shed.

I turned on the light of my cellphone and shone it ahead of me. There was a simple barrel bolt on the outside. I flipped it up and to the right and the door came bursting open as Amy spilled onto me.

"Oh, thank GOD ... AIR," she gasped.

And for a moment I didn't say anything, just wrapped my arms around her and squeezed her, taking in huge lungfuls of her as I stared wide-eyed into the distance. It was the longest hug I'd ever given her, and it was on the occasion of her kidnapping, which had been my fault.

Way to go, Chase! You dipshit.

# Chapter Twenty-Nine
## It's Just Something You Say

"Are you okay?"

"No, I am NOT okay!"

I know - it's a stupid thing to ask someone who has been abducted and locked in a tool shed, but it just came out.

"Let go! I need to breathe!"

She dropped to her knees and knelt, taking deep and deliberate lungfuls of air, interrupted by a couple of sneezes.

"I'm so sorry. I've never been so scared."

"*You've* never been so scared? Tell me about it."

"Well, first when I got to the ..."

"That does NOT mean tell me about it! It means that I am the one who gets to say that, not you."

"Sorry."

"Sorry? Sorry doesn't do it, Chase. Why is that guy so pissed at you? What did you do?"

"I didn't DO anything."

"Well, that twisted asshole Mike seems to think you did."

"Tell me what happened - tell me ... what he did to you."

"He locked me in a stinking shed for four hours, that's what he did."

"How? I mean ..."

"He pulled up alongside of me as I was walking home and said that he already had you and that if I didn't go with him, he'd get on the phone to his friend and have him cut off a finger."

I looked at her wide-eyed.

"Yes, it was stupid. No, I won't ever do it again. But you know what it's like to be scared for someone else, right? Before I knew it, we were here, he had my phone and I was shoved into this box. Now that you know everything there is to know - *what* did he *want* from you?"

"Whatshisname's skull."

"He already had it."

"No … I mean, I gave him the other stuff, but I kind of …"

"You held out? Really? How did you think that was going to work out?"

"I kind of thought it might go fairly well. I'd have the incriminating evidence and Mom would be … almost safe."

"No, Chase. That's not how it's going to go. Not with Mike. That guy is cold and hard. OhmyGOD I can't believe you yanked on his chain like that."

"Are you two okay? Need any help?" shouted a voice from the street. Somebody walking his dog had seen us crouching there, all stressed, tensely talking.

"Umm, no. Thanks," I replied. "We're alright. And we're on our way home." I stood up and waved at the guy and he walked off. I had the sense not to put a hand out to help Amy up. Figured I'd get smacked. Felt like I deserved it.

She got to her feet and I remembered I had her cellphone. I passed it to her and we walked the way I had come, back to the LRT station. She read the back-and-forth messages Mike had sent and got a pinched, pained expression I had never before seen on her face.

"He's afraid of you."

"What? I don't think so."

"Look at all the trouble he went to - he doesn't want to meet with you face to face again."

"That's silly. Why not?"

"Maybe he's afraid that you're going to get creative." A train rattled by on the nearby track as we approached the crisp lights of the station.

"Creative? Like with GareBear?"

"Maybe he figures that he'll be next on your list."

"I didn't kill GareBear - Mom did."

"Right. And Big Don ended up dead because ...?"

"Because he was clumsy and fell in front of a train. Or Mom pushed him."

"The athlete got clumsy. Or the woman who needed him to say alive and pay her back murdered him."

"I don't know - but it wasn't me."

The wind was still stiff and we both had to bend into it, keeping our arms close to our bodies to preserve body heat.

"My dad's gonna wonder where I've been."

"Just call him now. Say you're with me and we're doing a group project. That one always works."

"I'll send a text. It's easier to lie in a text."

"Or pretend you're someone else."

When she finished she put the phone in her back pocket. We stood shivering on the platform to catch the number 51 bus to get us home. Amy hugged herself to keep warm and I stuck my hands in my pockets.

"So, thanks," she said.

"For what?"

"Coming to get me."

"Least I could do."

"Yeah."

The bus came and we gratefully climbed on board and took seats at the back.

As we rode in silence, I considered a few things. Mostly Amy's leg against mine. That took most of my attention until we got off. She went her way with a wave. No smile. I was dying for a smile, but that was my problem and the smile stayed in her reserves where she could use it, when someone deserved it.

I trudged home, each step heavy with doubt and regret. The more I searched for desired outcomes, the more I realized that we were no longer free people.

Mike had found it easy to grab Amy and threaten her life. He had the goods to blackmail Mom or put her in jail. We didn't have any money anymore. Mike would make Mom steal from Mrs. Leckey. Mom wouldn't do it. Nothing good was going to happen.

And then there were all of my plans to have a life. Seemed comically stupid now.

Skinny, twisted, cold Mikey was an existential threat to everything I cared about.

Mikey had to go.

I asked myself a question.

What would Mom do?

# Chapter Thirty

## My Life as a Snitch

I punched the numbers starting with 613.

Seven more and then a four-digit extension.

There are no clicks, no static, no elevator music, and no ring tone.

Just an almost-familiar voice.

Thinking outside of the box.

That's what the wannabe bright lights say. It's such a cliché now that even saying it counts as thinking inside that box, being trapped in it and having nothing helpful to add.

I was trying to think outside of an old athletic bag. Full of the bones of the guy who gave me half my DNA and whose life ambition was to commit murder-suicide. I guess he got part of what he wanted. I might not do as well.

Where was that bag?

I thought I knew where Mikey lived because I had delivered him Whathisname's bones once before, but it was unlikely he kept the bag there. Unless he was as stupid as he looked. But he didn't seem to be - he got the better of both Amy and me. Gary was a breeze by comparison, a convenient, undemanding stationary target, his greasy self completely vulnerable to any plan I might have imagined.

That's why I had to keep spying on Kelly. I was a little disappointed when she changed the password on her phone. A shocking lack of trust. But she sucked at privacy, so I just over-the-shouldered it when she was distracted and snagged the new one.

I didn't like doing it, but if she wasn't going to be free and open with me, I had no choice. It was a good rationalization, and I kept it close to me. And I sure as hell wasn't going to be free and open with her.

Keeping on top of an increasingly difficult situation meant I had to find out when Mikey tried to contact her again. I knew he was going to. He went to a lot of trouble to get that skull and he was going to use it for the only purpose he could. I needed time. To find those damn bones. To reset The Plan. To get Mikey out of the way.

And it gradually came to me. My creative solution.

I identified myself.

"And what can *I* do for *you*?" A little sarcastic for a public servant I would have thought.

"You need to know something."

"Do I?" asked the Great Detective.

"Gary was threatening us."

"You already told me that."

"But I didn't give you proof."

"Okay. Do you have proof now?" I played the recording. The one where the GareBear threatened to cut me a new one.

"You recorded that?"

"Yup."

"Why?"

"I wanted to show Mom how dangerous Gary was. I'm sure he threatened her the same way."

"I didn't hear him threaten her ..."

"Gimme a break," I cut him off before he could get any more stupid. "He says, 'As soon as I'm finished with you, I'll take care of Kelly.' How is that not a threat? And that's the only one I have recorded. It got way worse."

"And why are you letting me listen to this now?"

"You need to see that she was acting in self-defense."

There was a long pause at the other end of the phone. "You'll send me that conversation. Right now." He wasn't asking very nicely, but I knew that's what he would want. I sent it off after I hung up and began to make preparations for the fallout.

I know I was taking a chance. I thought that if she was faced with a higher level of police attention there would be no opportunity for Mike to pressure her. If Mike thought that the cops were on to her, he'd back off. And if Mom thought they were going to arrest her anyway, she wouldn't give in to blackmail.

There were other risks. Mom could, probably would, lose her job. All the cops had to do was ask a few pointed questions to her employer and they'd drop her. The lady she took care of, Mrs. Leckey, might have something to say about it, because she loved Mom, but she'd be in for a rough ride.

And that had to be good. If Mom lost her job, no one could pressure her into stealing from the old lady. Mike would lose his grip on her. And without income, there would be no cash to hand over, no matter what. Sure, there would be a domestic crisis, but I could work more, we wouldn't starve or lose our home. For a while.

And in the meantime, I would gather resources, get creative, and remove Mike from our lives.

Blue-sky thinking, some people call it. More like wine-dark.

# Chapter Thirty-One

### Yes, That Was Stupid

Detaining me was a big mistake.

They had no evidence. It was just a big fishing expedition.

I guess I might have expected it, but my interpretation of things had to deal with reality, when Reynolds just got to make stuff up because his brain wasn't big enough to discover the truth on its own.

They took me in.

They searched my room. They searched our house. They took my phone. They took DNA samples. They went through all of my messages, contacts, histories and emails. They made me sit and wait in a little holding cell for hours. This was all something they should have done a long time ago, but their case was so weak that they weren't allowed, I'm sure.

And they had nothing.

Nothing.

Except what I had given them.

They thought the recording of my late-night heart-to-heart with Gary made ME the more likely suspect. Because he had accused ME of poisoning him, because he had directly threatened ME and because I had everything I needed to do him in - means, motive and opportunity.

Pure circumstantial bullshit.

They were missing the point entirely. They were supposed to go after Mom, to turn up the heat on her and help me get rid of Mikey. There wasn't anything directly implicating her, but Gary's murder fit her whole pattern, the one where she cleverly murders someone she's involved with in some way. One, two, three people, and if I didn't get out and get busy, you could be sure that Mike was next. Not that anyone would miss him.

This time when they questioned me, I had a lawyer. Not that I wanted one.

Because I was stupid. Lawyers are awesome!

Or at least mine was. Mom had been at work, and couldn't get away quickly, so she found me legal representation. I think she was massively pissed that I had given the recording to the cops and didn't want to be stuck trying to get me out of trouble herself. Better to spend all of our money on a lawyer, a punishment all by itself.

And she was worth it. Alexa Umoego was her name and she was about fourteen months pregnant. She was tired-looking, uncomfortable standing, sitting or doing just about anything. And she was sharp. Really sharp.

"Let me see if I am understandin' everything," she said in a soft accent, probably from West Africa, although I didn't ask. "Some poor excuse of a man dies of anaphylactic shock, a couple weeks after leavin' the home he shared with Chase. And you are blamin' his death on the people he terrorized, on the minor, no less, he had threatened with grievous bodily harm."

"We haven't charged him yet," Reynolds answered.

"And you're not goin' to." It was hard to decide whether that was a command or a statement of fact.

"What about the fingerprint we found?"

"What about it?"

"It's Chase's. It was found in the room that Mr. Twolan stayed in. And it was in peanut oil. A perfect thumbprint in peanut oil," Reynolds said looking me square in the eye. He sounded triumphant, like the final statement was definitive proof of my guilt.

"Ha! You've no timeline! Chase had a peanut butter sandwich yesterday and then went into that room to fetch a dishtowel."

"Is that his story?" He said it as if I wasn't in the room, even though he was still staring at me.

"It's no story," I said.

"Now Chase, you still should not be speakin'. These people do not have your interests in mind. They can't solve their crime, if they even have one, and they're lookin' to bully you into speakin' falsely." She turned to Reynolds. "And may I add that he willingly gave you, *offered* you, the recording you used to get a search warrant? Did you inform the judge of that? And now you have dragged him down here, threatened him with a murder charge, all because of an oily print that he may have left there anytime in a span of several weeks?"

Reynolds remained silent. He chewed his moustache and glared at me.

"Have you a charge, signed off by the Crown attorney? Are you proceeding with this farce? I'm sure there are other things we'd all rather be doing."

More silence. Chew chew chew.

"Well, then, we'll be leaving. Come now, Chase, give me a boost," she said as she extended a hand forward for me to grab. I helped her out of her chair and, as no one made any move to stop us, we walked out of the holding area and out towards the street.

"Thank you! You were great!" Hanging around in that little room was SO annoying. Such a waste of time that at one point I almost just got up and left. Probably not a good idea, but they were pissing me off.

"That's alright, dear. You know, they weren't very serious. I think they expected you to talk with them again unrepresented, like you did last time." She stopped and patted me on top of the head three times, none too gently. "Say it with me, now - that was stupid!"

"That was stupid," I repeated.

"And never again be offerin' the police anything, do you understand? Let them find their own misleading evidence. Thanks be to God that your mother has more sense! And she must not speak to them alone again, either. Do you hear me?"

"Yes."

"Excellent. Now, please take this." She gave me a stack of paperwork and her purse and a huge bright smile. "Help me to my car, will you? I must go home and put my feet up."

I only hoped she was going to make it home. Maybe she wasn't as pregnant as she looked, but I had to wonder why she was still working. Not that I wasn't grateful. I needed to get out. I had SO many things to do. I had been ignoring, like, ALL of my schoolwork and that catches up with you. I had another shift in Customer Disservice tomorrow and we needed the money now more than ever. And my scheme to take Mike's power away had blown up in my face.

I counted life suckages on my fingers as I found a bus home. Mom's pissed off. Cops are salivating at the chance to charge me. Behind in school. Work sucks. My dog is not getting enough attention and is starting to poop in the basement. The Plan is pretty much ruined.

Good thing my friends were still there for me.

# Chapter Thirty-Two

## Now I'm Even Worth Less.

8:45 in the morning.
**Me**: Amy?

10:30, when it was clear she wasn't coming to ComTech.
**Me**: Yoo Hoo! Skipping school today?

11:55, when I couldn't find anyone to have lunch with.
**Me**: What's going on?

3:20, after a day on my own without one friendly word to one friend-like person.
**Me**: If you don't talk to me, how will I know what I did wrong?

A few minutes later I was on the phone calling Rich. I was surprised not to have seen him at school, but it wasn't all that unusual.

"Stop right there," Rich said. "I'm not allowed."

"Whattaya mean you're not allowed?"

"What I said." His voice sounded stressed out over the phone, like he couldn't quite believe what he had to say. "The cops have been here talking to me and my parents. About you."

"Holy shit."

"Yeah - holy shit. And now my parents have said that while they don't think you're a murderer or anything like that, maybe I shouldn't hang around with you until this all passes over, until the police no longer have you on some suspect board with all kinds of arrows pointing at you. So you can forget whatever it is you're calling me about."

"What did they ask you?"

"About you and your mom and Gary. About when and where we've been hanging out. About what you say and do. They are totally in love with you."

"What did you tell them?"

"The truth. I said you didn't like Gary, but that nobody did. That you wanted your mom to date a better class of person. And that we hang out, eat lunch and play video games. Simple."

"I wonder if they talked to Carter."

"No idea - I didn't mention him and neither did they."

"Was it the moustache detective?"

"Who's that? It was a woman. Tremblay? Something like that. And what were you calling about, anyway. In case it's good enough to make me wanna sneak out."

"Oh, it was ... great, we ... I mean I was going to ask if, like we could majorly ..." I gave up and he jumped in.

"You don't want to do anything, right? This is somehow about Amy."

"Yeah. She's ghosting me."

"Really? Not her style I would have thought."

"I did something stupid and she kinda paid a price and I'm afraid she's still pissed at me."

"Did you try to kiss her?"

"Shut up."

"Worse? Feel her ..."

"Shut UP!"

"Hey, the whole boyfriend-girlfriend thing is a minefield, I should know. Just apologize and sound like you mean it."

"She's not my girlfriend and I already apologized. Just ... if you see her, tell her that I need, I mean, that I'd like to talk to her."

I poked my phone and tried to get in touch with Carter. I hadn't seen him either and the notion that the detectives were questioning Carter was alarming. Unlike Rich, he never actually talked on the phone and it took multiple tries to get him to answer a text.

**Me**: Hey!
**Carter**: S'up?
**Me**: What a relief. U OK?
**Carter**: Course! You?
**Me**: A little stressed. The cops talk to you?
**Carter**: Yup.
**Me**: What did you say?
**Carter**: I didn't answer any questions they didn't ask ;) After that, the truth. I don't know anything about anything.
**Me**: Seen Amy?
**Carter**: No. Cops must be talking to her, too. Bet it's hitting the fan, what with her dad and everything.
**Me**: Right.
**Carter**: Gotta go.
**Me**: One thing - delete this conv. OK?
**Carter**: Done.

I had no idea if Carter was as calm as he seemed. He had totally done me a solid by keeping his mouth shut about our little forest adventure. He was sticking his neck out. I was faking like I was all good with everything but I was freaking, having completely missed the fact that Amy's dad was a Crown-type attorney. The police interviewing his daughter about her friend's murdering mom might come up in dinnertime conversation. Worse, now they were accusing me.

"What's this about Chase being a murderer, pumpkin?" Amy's dad would say over his evening double scotch and soda. "I always thought he was too ugly for you but I know we didn't raise you to be consorting with killers. Now all the other Crown Attorney-types are making fun of me at work. Better not to see him anymore, or I will be forced to tell your mother. And lock you up in a tower."

And her mother would probably impale me with a stiletto heel.

Worse, Amy might never talk to me again.

I was getting seriously down until I remembered that going to get Whathisname's bones had been Amy's idea. She wasn't a simple innocent bystander, but a co-conspirator in the cover-up of one of Mom's murders. Mr. Crown Attorney Stone had better be careful about how vigorously the issue got pressed or his little dumpling would find herself in the soup along with me.

I felt better for about ten minutes.

Then, on my way to work, I considered that he would be much more likely to be even more curious than the police were. If Mr. Stone thought he had to protect his daughter, Amy's connection wasn't going to protect me. It was going to ruin me. Or Mom.

I was in a shitty mood behind the Customer Disservice Desk. And so what? Who's going to blame me if I didn't give a crap about price-matching soup, or scratch-and-sniff lottery tickets or expired coupons or any of the other meaningless interactions I was forced to endure.

Not Arjun. He's way too nice. He did ask me if everything was okay and I grunted that it was. My list of life suckages had grown and I was really tempted to dump them on him, see if he could avoid sharing my unhappiness.

Dead Dad.

Murderer Mother.

Alienated Amy.

Unwelcome at friends' houses, unable to deal with the existential danger to my life posed by Mike, and unlikely to affect change, I was as worthless as Hamlet. But as useless as he was, at least he was a prince. I was an animator who couldn't draw, a son whose father tried to kill his mother, a skinny kid in a black golf shirt with *Grocery Barn* stitched in big red letters across the left sleeve. Coming from nowhere and going nowhere.

The lottery machine made its stupid fakey happy music.

"Congratulations," I said to her. "You've won another lottery ticket.

"One more chance to win fuck all. Stupid fucking people and their stupid fucking worthless lottery tickets."

She claimed I said those exact words. When she complained about me to the manager.

No way. Not me. I don't use that kind of language. She was pissed that I didn't smile and say a glad, "Thank you very much it was my pleasure serving you!"

Arjun tried his best but I was fired.

They let me keep the shirt, though.

# Chapter Thirty-Three
## A Pariah Has a Lot of Quiet Time

The bright side of all the shitty things happening was that the universe was running out of fun things to do to me. It also meant that I had time to catch up with schoolwork, which wasn't the first circle of hell, like it sounds. Once you get into it and get things done, it's not so bad. What's truly bad is getting behind and never having time to do anything and simultaneously feeling guilty and stupid.

And now that I felt like I understood Hamlet, given my ass was as ineffectual as his ass, I found that I could breeze through an essay about him. And yes, I argued that he wasn't indecisive, philosophical, avenging, or ironic, but that he was massively useless.

It was all so easy with no friends. Or at least none who could be seen in public with me. And after a while I stopped trying to text Amy. No reply in ten days means that she's not going to, and I'm in danger of some sort of harassment charge if I keep it up.

Loki got walked more. He stopped pooping indoors, which was a good first step in seeing that the row house got cleaner. I was able to keep better track of Mom and her various social media, email, and bank accounts. She wasn't doing much more than me. Work work work.

Even my friends in the police service were giving me the cold shoulder. I was torn between my genuine desire to experience relief and my suspicion that it was only a temporary lull in what was becoming a long game for them. I wondered if they'd run out of gas or maybe found something better to investigate, like a crime against a victim way more sympathetic than Gary.

I discovered the truth from an unexpected source. Enlightenment was preceded by a joyful wash of relief, brought by a horde of butterflies in my stomach. They were visiting because of what I found during lunch hour one day in the side pocket of my backpack, the one I carry around school so that I don't have to go to my locker. I don't know how long it had been there, maybe days, before I found it and I nearly threw it away thinking it was some leftover scrap of a forgotten assignment. Then I noticed the handwriting.

*Hey Moron,*

*Thanks to you my phone has been taken away and my emails are being monitored. So I get to do what I swore when I was eight years old that I would never EVER do, and pass notes to a boy in school.*

*There is only one reason you are not in jail right now. A charge sheet came across Dad's desk with your name on it, and Dad had to recuse himself from signing because he knows you, you're my friend, and I guess that introduced a bias that's not allowed. Anyway, the delay in getting it to a new Crown attorney was long enough for some other evidence to be found that doesn't fit with the cops' theory of the crime, so they had to hold off.*

*So be careful! Stop doing stupid things!*

*I am forbidden (and yes, Dad even used that word like it's 1862 all of a sudden) from speaking with you. So you can reply by passing a note to Jenn. She'll get it to me.*

*Hang in there,*

*Love, Amy*

Love. She wrote love! I know she also called me a moron, but since when is a moron not loveable? She doesn't hate me, I wanted to scream.

And now I had a way of bringing myself back from Siberia, a slim opportunity to reconnect with Amy. Maybe all my other friends were there around the corner and maybe even my mother would start talking to me again soon, if only they could see that Amy had forgiven me, that Amy was still on my side, and that Amy had reached out to give me information and even invited further communication.

I scribbled a quick note, thanking her for the news and promising to stay in touch and ran to find Jenn. She spent most lunches in the art room, a place a guy like me should have spent more time, but which was a little like walking through an unfamiliar neighbourhood, one where everyone knew I didn't belong. I found her bending over the sink washing out some brushes.

"Hi, Jenn," I said awkwardly, out of breath from my run across the building and up the stairs. "Could you give this to Amy for me?" I held out the folded note.

"Aren't you too cute? Notes? Very retro." Jenn was about six foot two and maybe 103 pounds, all elbows and fingers. Her art was to paint small, detailed canvases, the sort of thing that you had to approach and examine really closely. She looked down at me intensely, trying to interpret me with a similar up-close gaze.

I guess Amy hadn't told her why we were exchanging notes instead of texts, so I just said, "Yeah - old school. It's a relationship experiment. We figure that the lack of immediacy will change the message - you know, the medium is the message, and all that."

"A relationship? That's new." I thought I was done for then, that she'd ask questions about what sort of relationship someone like me could have with someone like Amy. But that bullet remained unfired. "Okay." She put the note in her own backpack which was resting on a stool. "Not sure *I* would do that, though. Notes are not secure - anyone can read them."

You know, I hadn't even considered that. It made me sweat a bit as I wondered if I'd written anything revealing. I didn't think so and left it at that, said a big thanks and left.

For now, it was enough that I was communicating with Amy again. I went through the afternoon feeling better than I had in days, determined to get whatever I could onto the best track possible and then see where it all went. Maybe having reached a trough, there was nowhere to go but up.

Maybe.

# Chapter Thirty-Four

## The Enemy of My Enemy Is My Mother

My overall wretchedness gave Mom a sense of satisfaction. A job well done.

I deserved it, right? It was a price I was willing to pay, maybe even an investment if you want to continue with the stupid metaphor. The cost of freedom.

My misery eventually triggered her latent maternal guilt and set in motion a thaw which opened up a modest line of communication. We talked about TV, movies, school. And Amy, but only in the context of Mom asking me if I'd seen her, which I actually hadn't. I almost got the feeling that Mom had - seen her - and was holding back something. Weird.

Relieving some tension on the home front was important. I was keeping her in the dark about, like, everything and she was definitely keeping things from me. So there was a lot of silence, many things left unsaid, half-formed sentences that hung in the air like leaky helium balloons as we performed daily rituals.

Then Shotgun Mikey began to exercise his leverage once more.

Old-fashioned telephone calls were the most difficult things for me to keep track of as I spied on Mom's communication, and that seemed to be Mike's preferred way of blackmailing her. Mom would get phone calls on our single-handset landline, the one we kept for work, family, and school, the one she kept in her room. No way I could listen in. She got two or three calls like that while I was around and who knows how many when I wasn't. All I could do was wait, watch, and wonder until she asked me one fateful question. It was on a Tuesday morning, just before I tried to head to school, early for once.

As soon as my backpack got slung over my shoulder and I stepped toward the door, she asked, "Why does he call you the Dipshit?"

You have to give her credit, my clever mother, because she caught me so off guard that I almost answered the question.

"What? Who?"

"Mike Lawrence. Why does he call you the Dipshit?"

"Why does he call me anything?"

"It seems like the two of you have met."

"It was Gary's pet name for me." Not a bad lie to avoid the issue. It could've been true.

"He said he had a story to tell me. About you."

"I wouldn't believe anything that guy says."

"So you've met him?"

Shit. Careful, Robinson!

"No - I don't have to meet a blackmailing creep like him to not trust him." And back to the offensive. "You're the one who seems to hang out with criminals, not me. What's with all the questions - has he started making threats again?"

"Mmm. And this time he claims to have ..." She paused and peered at the middle distance as if the next part got stuck in her throat. "... your father's, I mean Whatshisname's, remains. He says he ... went for a walk in the woods and found ... them. Says Gary told him where to go."

I'm glad she wasn't looking at me. I should have been shocked, horrified, nauseated, something. But I was none of those. I could only be apprehensive, waiting for the next part where I was challenged about my role in Whatshisname's excavation.

"Really?"

It was about the dumbest thing I could have said.

"Yes, Robinson. Really." She looked me in the eye, looked at me hard, looked at me for any sign that I might know something I should not know, that I had done something I should not have done, that I was someone she could not trust. If she knew that I'd been chief bones handler she wasn't letting on. And neither was I.

"Wait ... what's he going to do with them?"

"Take them to the police. Or tell the police where to find them, more like."

"Unless you ...?"

"First he wanted cash - you know, the five hundred I was going to make from Don before the train ... hit him, five hundred to keep quiet about what I'd told Gary, about that night in the forest. Now, he wants what Gary wanted - for me to steal from Mrs. Leckey. She's a rich old lady, from a generation who liked collecting jewellery. That's what he thinks, anyway."

"Is he right?"

"I guess she has some, not as much as Mike thinks."

"What are you gonna do?"

"I don't want to steal from a dotty old lady. It's why I gambled all that money on Don."

Yeah, right.

If Don was important, then why did she kill him? And then, killing Gary and Don, not to mention Whatshisname, she could do, but she didn't want to steal from a wealthy octogenarian, from someone who would never know the difference?

An interesting set of choices. But I kept my mouth shut.

"Now Mike wants me to deliver him a sample, a down payment he calls it, today. He's got a connection that will appraise its value. I need you to go, I need you to do it for me. This is just the first. If it's high quality and there's more, then we make an exchange. The rest for the ... remains."

"Why me?"

"Because I can't be there at the time he says."

"Why not?"

"Never mind - I just can't be there. Can you just do this for me?" She sounded annoyed like I was a lazy kid trying to get out of shovelling snow. And it worked.

"I can," I said immediately. She grabbed my right wrist and turned it over so my palm was up to receive the small wood and velvet box she smacked into it. "Take this - it was my grandmother's and I was told it's valuable. Mike is going to text me a location later and I'm going to text you. All you do is go and hand it over. That's all."

"But what are you accomplishing besides giving him your grandmother's ..." I paused to open the box. "Necklace?" Inside was a fine silver chain and a large pear-shaped jewel - something red and not a diamond - attached to it.

"I gain some time. I'll be able to figure my way out of this, but I have to put Mike off for a few days. It'll be worth it."

That had to be a lie. She's sending *me*, putting *me* at risk just for a few days' delay? Even though I wasn't afraid of Mikey in the slightest (more like I wanted to bash his Camaro moustache through the back of his head), Mom had to have a better reason. Did she think I was stupid?

"I'm supposed to take this to school?" was all I said.

"You have to - I'm not sure when he'll call. He's being very cagey, like he wants to keep us guessing until the last possible moment. He's probably afraid we'll set him up."

Maybe he was afraid Mom might chuck him in front of the nearest moving vehicle, or find a way to bash his brains in or deliver a little poison along with the fancy jewel. I know I was considering all of those things.

I stuffed the box into my backpack, agreed to keep my eyes open for texts and assured Mom I wouldn't let anything delay me from making any rendezvous she arranged.

It's a five-minute run to school from our place, one I had done often enough. This time because there was one place I had to go before dashing to my back-of-the-class seat in math, I came in under four minutes, a new record. I tore through the now-thinning crowds in the halls to the art room, outside of which I knew Jenn and all the other art room rats had lockers. One person was there closing a locker door.

"Which locker is Jenn's?" I demanded.

"No idea," he said, a what-have-we-here look pickling his face. He pointed across the hall and into a classroom. "She's right there?" he sneered, like I was particularly thick as well as unworthy. Asshole.

Jenn was sitting in the front row of a class, just two seats from the door. I frantically got a notebook out of my backpack, scribbled a few words, folded it and wrote AMY in large letters on it. I walked to the threshold of the door and chucked it at Jenn.

If I startled her, she didn't show it. She looked at the paper, spied me outside the door looking at her pleadingly. She looked at the note and at me and smiled broadly, like she thought I was kitten-cute.

"Okay," she mouthed at me.

I felt like a twelve-year-old passing notes. No matter, I just needed her to deliver the message. I snuck and groveled my way into math and pretended to listen to Mr. Bradley take up homework that I hadn't finished. Gradually, I calmed down. My breathing slowed, my sweat dried, and I tried to focus on the regular routine of a school day. Deep down, though, I was a coiled spring, one hand waiting on my cellphone for the telltale vibration of a text message, one knee jumping up and down under my desk, my mind jumping from the message I had just sent to the one I might receive any second.

# Chapter Thirty-Five
## Oh, THAT'S What It Is.

11:45 and still no message from ... anyone. The bell chimed and I didn't know where to go. So, I paced back and forth, up and down, left and right past the main office in the hall, looking like a lost obsessive-compulsive puppy, I'm sure.

*The turkey flies at midnight.*

That was my message. To Amy.

I had so little time, I thought that maybe if I wrote something quixotic enough, ambiguous enough - okay, stupid enough - that maybe she'd find me and we could talk. I also had to write something that Jenn could read, because I knew she would, and not understand at all.

So, the turkey was flying.

And my pocket was vibrating.

**Mom**: The Holzman bridge. One hour. Enter from the north. I'll call the school and sign you out.

**Me**: Holzman ... bridge?

**Mom**: Pedestrian bridge over the Queensway. Brand new - remember the whole 8 lanes were closed when they put it in overnight?

**Me**: Yup. Got it. On my way.

Great. A half-hour walk. I started running down the hall, stopping near the front entrance just long enough to make sure that I still had the necklace. I reached into my backpack, gripped the box and was about to sling my backpack over my left shoulder and dash out when a familiar voice temporarily washed all purpose from me.

"Forget midnight, it looks like the turkey is on its way right now."

"It's Amy," was all I could say.

"And it's Chase," she replied. "And Chase has lost his mind."

"I have? Oh, the note! The turkey - it worked - you found me!"

I know I was babbling, but I didn't want to see her then. I wanted to talk to her later, after my meeting with Mikey was over. Maybe that's what I should have said.

"Yeah, I had to spot the hot-and-bothered weirdo pacing the halls. Only you could send out an S.O.S. so bizarre."

"Great - but I have to go."

"Where?"

She looked so mind-blowing in just a flannel shirt and jeans and I could see her clavicle and everything and I wanted to stay and talk and hug and maybe even talk some more if she got tired of hugging. And I had to ditch her.

If I told her, she might want to come. If I didn't tell her, she might insist. I thought about refusing to answer, lying, just running away, but I had brought this on myself with the note. Besides, she was faster than me.

"Rendezvous with ... someone."

"You're meeting ... a new girlfriend? Is that what this is about - you need advice?"

"NO!" I said a little too forcefully. "I mean, no, it's not like I have a line of girlfriends waiting for me and I have to skip school to see them all."

"It might be worth it."

"Did you ever skip to meet BOB?"

"Bob's a jerk."

What? Was there a sliver of hope that Amy had got rid of one of the impediments to my eternal happiness? She didn't give me a chance to ask.

"If you're skipping school this must be serious. Tell me or I'll hold you here." She grabbed my backpack and pulled it toward her."

"Okay, you win. I have to meet Mike. Shotgun Mike."

"Mike the Dickhead Kidnapper?" she corrected, letting the pack go and almost sending me backwards on my butt.

"I really don't have a lot of time," I said as I moved toward the door, hoping she'd leave me alone to go get killed or whatever. I turned and slammed open the heavy fire door, and took the concrete steps outside two at a time.

"Wait! You don't understand! You can't!"

At the bottom of the stairs I turned to look up at her. "I *have* to."

"But there's something you don't know!"

"There are a *lot* of things I don't know!" I jogged off and glanced over my shoulder to see her descending the stairs as if to chase me. "You can tell me I'm wrong later! But I can't be late!" And I took off.

I probably had enough time to walk, but I couldn't make myself slow down. I paid the price. October had turned the corner from red to brown, from warm colours and sunny skyscapes to crunchy leaves and blustery winds, gusts in my face, skin-cracking dryness pouring down my neck. Jogging for long enough, though, still brings on a sweat, one that makes you cold without ever passing through cool.

About four minutes after I got to Harmer Avenue and the bridge, too early to expect Mike to appear, my armpits, crotch and for some reason the back of my neck were wet and freezing. My ears were achingly cold from facing the wind, completely different from frostbitten wintery lobes.

My sweaty self would soon start shivering. I hunched my shoulders and tried to bury my neck into my completely inadequate jacket. After briefly rifling through my backpack, my fists were in my pockets, the right one clutching the velvet-covered box Mom had given me this morning.

I figured I might as well get out of the wind, so I approached the enclosed pedestrian bridge, a straight, slightly arched span of glass and steel that didn't allow would-be jumpers to dive off or idiots to chuck stuff at cars flying by underneath. I went in just far enough to get out of the wind and keep an eye on the opposite entrance. I cooled further as I stood gazing at the freeway traffic beneath me, actually hoping to see Mikey's cheesy moustache and skinny slouch.

They say be careful what you wish for, right?

"I thought I was clear that I didn't want to see your dipshit face!" His voice, coming from a good twenty metres away, sounded like it was coming through a tube, which I guess it was.

I turned to face him. "Sorry to disappoint you!" I pulled the box out of my jacket pocket and held it up. "I guess if you don't want this, I'll just go home."

"Stay right there!" He walked closer, stopping about three metres away. "Throw it here!"

I pitched the box underhand to him and he caught it in both hands. He turned it over, opened it and stared blankly at the jewel necklace inside.

"There's more like this?"

"As far as I know."

"Alright. Now, what happened to your cute little mommy? I was lookin' forward to our rendezvous. Why isn't she here like I said?"

"Beats me. Women - who can figure 'em out, right?"

"You are quite the little bullshitter, kid. I'm telling you - next time you follow my instructions or there will be an unholy shitstorm to pay."

"What would a holy shitstorm look like - you know, if I had the choice to make?

I learned three things. The first was that Mike was faster than he looked. The distance between us decreased instantly and I found that one of his boney hands was holding me up by my neck. It wasn't quite one of those superhero chokeholds accomplished with the aid of camera angles and a winch, but he was strong for a skinny gun-toting pock-marked weenie-moustached loser from a land before time.

"It looks like this, Dipshit," he drawled as he shook me. Then he punched me in the balls and let me drop to the ground. "And if you don't want to see worse, next time do what I tell you."

So, that was the second thing. A holy shitstorm appeared to be characterized by choking and a blow to the testicles. Not sure if the choking part was necessary but I was fairly certain that the punch to my balls was sufficient. It did beg the question of what an unholy one would look like, but I got the idea. He walked off, not the same way he had entered but in the direction I had come from. I had one eye open, the other being on the ground and clenched in the same rictus of breathless pain as were my torso, arms, legs and fists.

The last time I had been reduced to this state was maybe in Grade 6 when a so-called friend had pretended to kick me in the crotch. He was a poor judge of distance and he made full contact. I had also been pretending - faking that I was not worried about him actually connecting. Too cool to move.

And then unable to move.

It wasn't any better six years later. And that was the third thing.

# Chapter Thirty-Six
## Pain Has a Way of Sharpening One's Resolve

No danger of generating one of those cold sweats on the way home. There are no buses that go from where I was to where I needed to go, so it was just a stagger, a limp and then a slow walk back to school, back to meet Amy because I said I would. I had very little company on my short-strided journey through Halloween-readied neighbourhoods. Nothing but grey skies, blowing leaves, and broken lines of tall yellow plastic markers proclaiming that Andy was going to remove snow from these driveways this winter. Plastic skulls gaped eyelessly at me from every other house, laughing at me and my little problems. I wasn't so keen on the seasonal decorations this year.

I tried to keep my eyes on the sidewalk ahead of me, to focus on each next step and to think about the next phase of my grudge-match with Mikey. He had got the better of me - again. It would be different next time.

And next time I would be prepared to do what had to be done to be free of this parasite who thought he was a predator. Because next time, there would be no next time. This had to end, even if I had to take a page from Mom's book.

No soliloquies, no navel-gazing.

No to-be-or-not-to-be procrastination.

I tried to get some idea of my appearance as I walked past parked cars. Even in the dim reflections, I could tell that I looked rough. I was hopeful that my walk might restore some colour to my face, make me appear something better than a zombie on a bad day for brain-eaters.

I mounted the concrete steps to the school slowly, deliberately, with a minimum of nauseating testicular jostling. She was waiting inside and came out to meet me.

"What happened to you?" Amy held her hand to her mouth like she was afraid she'd barf.

"Nothing." And then I added, all casual and cool, "Why do you ask?"

"Because you look like shit."

"Thanks."

"What happened?"

"I did what I was supposed to do. I met with Mikey and gave him what he wanted."

"What did he want?"

"Something from Mom."

"You don't know how stupid you are!"

"Whoa! Unfair! I have a pretty good idea." She grabbed my arm and pulled me just inside the heavy wooden double doors. I tried not to show how much it hurt to follow.

"They're watching him!" she whisper-shouted.

"Who's watching who?"

"HIM! The cops are watching that asshole Mike."

"How do you know?"

"They think he maybe killed Gary. The two of them had serious history according to Dad. That's why you're not in jail. They're watching *him*. And if they saw you with him, they're going to link you two and then make their way to your mom and Gary and who *knows* what."

"I doubt that they saw us just now."

"How do you know?"

"I just doubt it. We were ... hard to see." I tried to see my meeting with Mikey from the point of view of a cop. If they saw how it ended, wouldn't they have maybe helped me out, given me a ride home, or maybe to the hospital? At least they wouldn't suspect us of being accomplices or co-conspirators or, worse, Facebook friends. But the downside was obvious.

"I know what they'll find if they're any good at watching him - they'll find Whatshisname." I pictured Reynolds getting a search warrant and finding an athletic bag bulging with bones and a bashed-in smiley skull. That would get his moustache going like crazy.

"If you had waited I could have told you what I couldn't risk writing - why I'm not supposed to talk to you. I gave Dad a hard time, and I mean a CRAZY wild-eyed screaming hard time, about you when he said I couldn't have contact with you. He had to convince me that it was better for you if I didn't. That if you knew, you might do something instead of letting Mikey incriminate himself."

"But your dad doesn't know about Whatshisname - right?"

"Which is why I'm talking to you anyway. But it's too late. You went out and screwed up by yourself."

"Before you say anything else, let me say that I was only doing what I was asked to do - by a higher authority. She-Who-Gave-Me-Life, no less."

"Your mother set you up?"

"But she couldn't have known ..." And then I thought about it for a millisecond and remembered that she hadn't told me why she couldn't go to the meeting. Was she just making me go because she couldn't go herself or because she suspected the cops were watching? What sort of fiendish woman gave birth to me?

Or did I have it all wrong, and Mom was just afraid of Mikey - afraid for herself in the same way that she might have been afraid of Gary? And she sent me thinking that if I was in danger, it was a different kind.

That would be okay. It made me feel funny to think it, but I could handle that. At the same time, maybe it was just a vote of confidence - I could take care of myself. But so could she - she had proved that once, twice, maybe three times.

And maybe she was telling the truth, that she had to be somewhere so important that she needed me to go. I figured that was the least likely of the scenarios, though. What could be so important and yet so secret?

The question gave me my next step. I had to figure out where Mom had been and why she was keeping things from me. If my swollen boys had bought us time, I should be able to spin some kind of plan to set things straight.

Good guys over bad guy.

---

Protagonist over scrawny-but-deceptively-strong sociopathic douchebag.

I knew from deep inside my knowing place that I was going to need more than allies, I was going to need friends. Especially Amy. For so many reasons. I needed access to her - reliable and timely access.

"So - do we get to talk now? Not through Jenn Who-Thinks-I'm-Weird?" I motioned into the school, hoping to find somewhere to sit for a few minutes.

"She's okay. She just doesn't know you and your fascinating backstory and charming quirks."

"Fine with me." We walked slowly down the deserted after-school corridor, me trying not to limp and to stand straight.

"Just get someone else to call me - make sure your name doesn't come up on the call display. Maybe someday I'll get my phone back and you can text, but that might not happen for a few days yet. My mother is working on that for me. She's been all over Dad, claiming that taking my phone away was a move to keep me from communicating with her. And she likes you, mostly because you're such arm candy."

Arm candy? She couldn't have been talking about me. BOB would have been arm candy, BOB with nice teeth and lots of money to buy clothes that actually fit. Maybe BOB was gone, though, perhaps a victim of his own BOB-ness.

A wooden bench beckoned and I gingerly sat while Amy further explored a familiar theme - how funny her mother is. "No shit, she actually said, 'Do you hate me so much that you must sever my link with my only child? Drive a stake through my heart! Again? And that boy - he's a rake but otherwise harmless, can't you see?' It's beautiful - a full-blown three-act drama, and Dad may have to give in. I'll work on it."

"Your mother makes NO sense sometimes," I said, while noting that Amy's impression of her mother was almost perfect. Over-enunciated, mid-Atlantic actor-speak, theatrical gesticulations and all. And I had a brain flash. Over the phone, I'd bet no one could tell them apart.

A wash of multi-hued creative-moment drugs flowed from the back of my head to the front, and in their wake was born an idea. It was hard to catch at first, as every time I tried to seize its many implications and consequences, it seemed to bob away like an apple in a barrel.

After a time, though, after saying so long to Amy and making my evenly paced, gentle-if-not-graceful way home, I found that the idea was emerging, that I could grip it and peel it. Properly sliced and pitted, it would soon become a sweetly flavoured, fully formed scheme, replete with both risks and rewards.

Maybe some retribution, too.

# Chapter Thirty-Seven
## Kickin' It Old School

"How did it go? What happened to you?"

I didn't say anything, briefly wallowing in the power of teenage silence.

"Tell me what happened. I was worried!"

Really, she was worried *now* after sending me to the ball-busting parasite, King of the Low Blow and petty criminal confidante of Gary Too-Stupid-to-Carry-an-EpiPen Twolan?

Yeah, I guess I had become just a little resentful as I navigated my baby steps home. I had taken a shot to the family jewels just to give that asshole a family jewel, and I just wanted to know why. So, I replied as reasonably and rationally as I could.

"Were you? Worried?"

"Of course."

"No reason to be. All I had to do was fling a piece of jewellery at a sociopath."

"Did he say anything? Do anything?"

"All he did was ask if there was more. You've got him on a hook if that's what you want, if that's what all of this is about."

"What does *that* mean?"

"Nothing."

"Don't you *nothing* me. What did you mean?"

"Not anything."

"Right now, Robinson. Out with it."

"He was angry that I was there. He wanted to know where you were, and I could not tell him because of course, I did not know."

"What did he do? Are you okay?"

"I did not enjoy myself." I had to decide at that moment to test the honesty of our relationship - both mine and hers. My honesty was already hopelessly compromised, so I tested hers. "I was looking forward to my Com Tech class because we were going to learn how to blow each other up on film and instead I was exchanging unpleasant monosyllables with someone whose presence in our lives is clearly your fault. I just would like to know what's going on."

If she already knew what had happened, I should see a tell, an indication that she had reason to doubt my story.

Nothing.

"I was ... meeting with someone who might be able to help with all of this."

What? Someone? I couldn't believe this. She wasn't even bothering to make up a good lie.

"Who?" I demanded.

"I can't say."

"You can't or you won't?"

"Both."

So I gave her one of those looks that she liked to use on me, one of those that said, "I know you're lying and keeping things from me and I don't deserve to be treated like this and you're going to feel guilty for a long, long time."

Didn't work on her any better than it had ever worked on me. I gave up and went to lie down, relieve some painful pressure and grapple with reality for a while. Chase needed some Chase time.

I had been experiencing a significant failure of intelligence. Spying on She-Who-Gave-Me-Life was not working. How was I supposed to deal with the restoration of The Plan without adequate information? How could I be expected to take care of business if she actually succeeded in shutting me out of important details?

I mean, I'd seen her taxes (turns out if you don't make much you don't pay much), knew all of her investments (none after Don took them), gone had through all her pay stubs (shocking how the caring professions are underpaid), emails (a total snore), texts (mostly to me), you name it and she's getting away with meeting with yet another loser, just the latest in a line of losers who she was turning into a trail of bodies that even the dumbest cop was going to be able to follow. Was she just waiting to kill again? Was it some sort of disorder, syndrome, an addiction now? I could not possibly keep covering for her.

On the positive side, Mom's sacrifice of her grandmother's necklace might have bought me a useful delay. I had no job, my isolation had taken care of my homework, and Amy was almost back. I could prepare. No more hacking, or digital eavesdropping. I was ready to kick it old school.

The same time the next day, I had stashed under my bed in its box an old-fashioned plug-in-the-wall telephone. My room had a phone jack. The next time there was a strange call from a skinny lowlife blackmailing jerk-off, I would be able to listen in. Old school. I would also be able to disable the line by simply leaving it engaged, sending a busy signal to the world.

And with a little help from my friends, I might be able to convince Mike to bring Whatshisname's bones right here to us.

# Chapter Thirty-Eight
## Another Miracle of Evolution

"Halloween is one of the least weird things you people do," Carter told me, crunching down on a peanut-free chocolate Halloween treat as I used his phone. He used the term "you people" when he wanted to demonstrate how screwed up the "colonial culture" is. "At least one day of the year you think about the dead, maybe even your ancestors, and pay attention to the possibility of the existence of spirits out there affecting your lives."

"I wonder if that's what's going on, you know, with me and my mother and  Whatshisname? He's trapped in some sort of death-enabled revenge scenario, working with all his psycho-killer ghost buddies to ruin our lives because Mom kicked his ass."

"Can't rule it out," Carter replied sagely, popping another chocolate bar into his mouth.

"Is that what this is about?" Amy complained over the phone I was holding out on speaker mode. "Because I have better things to do."

"Nonono, don't go - we are gathered together here in sight of Carter so that he may witness and be amazed. Go ahead, give it your best shot."

"Okay - wait ..." There was a pause of a few seconds while she channelled, focused, or did whatever she did in order to achieve her magic.

"I ... need you to come tonight. My son, Chase ... won't be here. We can make the exchange and then I never want to hear from you again."

Carter's eyebrows lifted.

"Whattaya think?"

"That's good - she got the pauses and everything. Over the phone, I would never know that's not your mother."

"YES! You're beautiful! I mean, that was beautiful!" I gushed.

"Yeah, we all know what you meant," muttered Carter. I'm not sure if Amy heard him or not.

This was my acceptably effective method of contacting Amy. I invited friends over, a different friend or combination of friends whenever I needed to call her. They used their cellphones and my name never appeared on anyone's call display. I asked Rich and Carter and even Rich's girlfriend, who thought Amy and I had some sort of Romeo-and-Juliet thing going where our parents hated each other and took it out on us. I guess she was a quarter right - Amy's dad didn't want me hanging out with her, and her mom probably liked BOB better (and she had a point) but it wasn't like there was a blood feud going on. I think Mom missed having Amy around a lot but never pressed me about why she hadn't seen her. So, my friends visited and I used them shamelessly, feeding everyone Halloween treats, potentially depriving late-arriving free-loading ghouls who might show up on the thirty-first.

I was preparing to deal, creatively and finally, with Mikey. If my great-grandmother's necklace had been worth much, it may have provided the nudge necessary to bring to life a mature philosophy in Mikey's sloped forehead. As a human parasite that considers itself a predator, he will perceive his host/prey as dull-witted, slow-moving, incapable of escape or resistance. As long as he was as creepily confident as I thought he was, we'd be good. I think I had demonstrated just how helpless I was. Whether that had been my intention or not is irrelevant.

My own confidence was building. Keeping track of whether or not Scumbag Mike was trying to contact Mom was more problematic. I had to wait for calls on the landline and then slide into my room to listen in. I tried to leave the line connected to generate a busy signal for most of the day, but calls inevitably got through when I was not there or was unprepared. I went to Mom's phone and wrote the numbers down - several did not have a name associated with them - to try them out later, thinking I might luck out on the phone Dirtball Mike used.

What I needed to do now was to get Amy over here, contact the sleazeball on the phone and lure him into my carefully laid trap, all the while preventing any contact between She-Who-Gave-Me-Life and the man himself.

My window of opportunity was narrowing. My transparently secretive mother was showing signs of unsanctioned blackmail-related activity. She kept to herself, was away from home longer than could be explained by her work schedule, and seemed to be unusually concerned about my movements. There had been several phone calls that I could not prevent, several of them from two different numbers, neither of which I recognized.

That's why I had Carter over and why we were rehearsing with Amy. They had both met Dickhead Mike, and Amy especially had reason to want to see him put away. I needed them both.

Tomorrow would be Halloween.

Tomorrow, Mom was working.

Tomorrow, then, would be the designated day.

Amy would lie about where she was going after school.

She'd come here. She'd make a couple of phone calls.

I would hand out sugary treats at the door to ghosts, ghouls, pirates, princesses, mummies, and monsters. I'd wait for the final monster of the evening, a fully grown freakishly ugly monster of the shithead variety.

And I'd show him my costume. I'd spent hours on it, painting cardboard and rigging the main prop, which would light up from below. I would be a giant box of Sugar-Frosted Crap-ee-os. With a meat cleaver sunk into the middle.

I know. Predictable. But, being a cereal killer seemed to be in keeping with a family tradition.

# Chapter Thirty-Nine
## An Evening with the Dead

Surprise, the really disorienting kind, sucks ginormously when you're laying a trap for a morally handicapped human parasite.

"OHMYGOD!"

Yeah, that was Amy, who doesn't like to be surprised either.

"OH. MY. GOD!"

We were looking through the phone numbers that we had to use to lure Shotgun Mikey.

"What is it?" I asked for the fifth time.

"This one - this number - it's my dad's cellphone."

"Holy shit! Are you sure?"

"I *know* my dad's cell number."

"Why's he calling my mother?"

"How would I know?" Her tone was more than unsettled - she was as alarmed as I was. We silently stared at the list for what must have been an uncomfortably long time.

"Maybe they're dating," Carter piped in. We both looked daggers at him, each of us speechless with the implications. "Just sayin', you know, elephant in the room."

"Maybe he was just calling to make sure you weren't here."

"Checking up on me? He better not be."

"Maybe they were just general goodwill calls that a prosecutor makes to a murder suspect when his daughter is friends with her son."

"Don't be ridiculous."

"Then we're back to my dating theory - divorced dad, widowed well-put-together mom? Doesn't sound so insane now, does it?" Carter tapped the side of his forehead with one finger.

"Well, ... at least ..." I scrambled to find a way to finish that thought, anxious to get us off the subject. "At least we know we don't have to call that one. It makes this simpler in a way - the only other unknown number must be Mike's blackmailing phone."

"Right - simple," Amy said, voice dripping with sarcasm.

"It'll be simpler when you guys are brother and sister. I'll only have one house to visit. It'll be hard to choose, though. Amy's place is bigger, but I like this location."

The only way to shut him up was to get on with the plan. It was time-sensitive to begin with and now the horrible panicky stress I was feeling just made me more impatient to get busy. I had neither trapped nor cornered Gary, so this was a new experience in dealing with lowlife forty-somethings. I had tried to compensate by scripting the evening as carefully as I could.

First, get Mike here with the bones. After calming down, Amy used our home phone to call the second number. There was an answering machine - she read the lines I'd written for that circumstance.

"This is Kelly. It's ... today ... Halloween ... about five o'clock. I have what you want. It HAS to be tonight though. Call back." The anxiety she felt about the potential disaster-dating came through in her voice and if anything it made her sound even more like Mom.

"Brilliant," I said when she'd hung up.

"Yeah - nice!" Carter agreed. "Now what?"

"We wait, and do a couple of things in the basement."

Amy and Carter helped me move some boxes of Christmas crap out of the furnace room, the only space with an exposed concrete floor, and lay down a thick nylon tarp.

"Hey, Chase - you're not gonna cut up Mike's body here, or anything like that, are you?" Carter asked.

"No way!"

"Okay - just asking. Not like he doesn't have it coming to him, but I left my good skinning knife at home."

"I'm glad you asked. It was creeping me out," Amy said to him as we went back upstairs. "What are you ..." Almost on cue, as I was trailing them up the stairs, the phone rang. We crowded into the kitchen and looked at the call display.

"It's HIM. Here," I said to Amy, handing her the script.

"Yeah, hello." Again, it was perfect - that's the way Mom always answers the phone. Amy held the receiver away from her ear so that we could hear the other side of the conversation.

"Well, hello there yourself, *Kelly*. It is such a pleasure to hear from you so soon. Now tell me - why are you so anxious to see me today?"

"I just want ... to finish this. If we make the exchange tonight ... here ... no one will get in the way. I'm alone." I gave her two thumbs up for that last bit. It almost sounded like an enticement, as nauseating as that was.

"I agree - we don't want the dipshit to get between us, do we?"

"So ... you're coming? Maybe after the little kids are gone? About nine?"

"Alright. Alright. Lookin' forward to doin' ... *business* with you." And then he almost sang, a lascivious leer behind his words, "See you soon, darlin'," and the line went dead. Amy and Carter high-fived each other, but I felt as much like puking as celebrating, so neither came out.

He was on his way.

The next three hours dragged by. I handed out candy to trick-or-treaters with one hand while controlling Loki with the other. We fed ourselves a nervous meal of frozen pizza. After about eight o'clock, we turned the lights off and stayed away from the front door and all windows, just in case Mike showed up early and decided to sit and watch. If he got the scent of a trap, this would be all over before it started. We needed him to arrive at the front door expecting no one but Kelly, expecting nothing but an attractive woman half his size, a *well-put-together* target for blackmail and whatever else might occur to a predator who was thinking with his junk.

My stress levels got higher, my heartbeat louder and my hands got shakier as it got closer to nine. Before, during my first scheme to rid us of the Gary infestation, I didn't break a sweat. The difference was that while

Garebear had made a lot of violent threats, Creepy Mike had pretty much acted as much as threatened. He fought dirty and he was likely to show up armed.

If he brought more than his skinny self, even the shotgun, things might get interesting.

I sat and waited in the dark of the kitchen. Amy and Carter talked quietly about nothing. Each knew a little bit about my plans, but neither knew the whole thing. It didn't help that I had to keep improvising based on recent developments. It's not like anyone knows what they don't know. How could I be blamed on that basis? Then again, I guess I could blame myself for whatever reason or lack thereof I wanted to.

The doorbell shattered my inner dialogue. Loki barked as dogs do but I put him away in the guest bedroom with a new chew-toy to destroy. This part we'd rehearsed. I backed into the kitchen, Carter disappeared and after a moment, Amy shouted in her best Mom, "Door's open! Come in!" The front door handle turned and the door slowly swung open. Outlined on the threshold was a man holding a familiar athletic bag.

"Hello?" he called as he took a cautious step forward.

"Close the door, please ... I'll be right there. Just ... changing my clothes!" I had wanted her to say she was taking care of the dog, but she was ad-libbing, maybe hoping to tempt Lowlife Mikey into moving without caution.

I couldn't see him, but I'll bet his twisted little brain was considering his options. He may have been suspicious but the prospect of a rich haul of old-lady jewellery, as well as a chance to let his creepier fantasies come to life, drew him in.

As he closed the door and took the first two slow steps toward the kitchen, I showed myself. "Hey, Mike. Are you here for the unholy shitstorm?"

Maybe that was a bad idea.

I've said it before - this guy was quick. In less than a second, he had put down the bag, unzipped it and pulled out a short-barreled shotgun.

# Chapter Forty

## Seriously - No One Is Getting Dismembered

"Did you think you were going to surprise me, Dipshit?" He levelled the weapon at me, not two metres away. The barrel looked unnaturally wide from this perspective.

"Not really," I replied. "I thought I might leave that for someone else."

The front closet door slid wide with a swoosh and Carter brought down something on the back of Mikey's head with a hollow, crowd-pleasing thud. His head jerked backwards and then his body collapsed forward onto the floor. I was impressed.

"Nice!"

"I always said that the only thing a math textbook is good for is hand-to-hand combat. Turns out I was right." Carter threw the book on the floor while I stepped over Mike and pulled the shotgun out of his hand. Mike started to swear violently as he gripped the back of his head.

"Couldn't you have hit him harder?" Amy asked as she came out of the kitchen behind me.

"These guys have a low ceiling. No room to wind up."

"Just as well. We need him conscious for now. Let's get him downstairs." Amy was about to grab an arm and Carter was holding out his hand to take charge of the weapon when I had an idea. "I think Amy should have the shotgun. Mikey here needs to know that it's being aimed by someone who truly would like to pull the trigger."

"You got that right," Amy said as I handed it to her.

"It looks ready to shoot," Carter commented. "Just pull the trigger, and beware of the kick. And of the fact that everything in front of you is going to be blown away."

"Sounds good." She pointed it at the floor as Carter and I pulled him onto his feet and forced him down the stairs, Carter twisting an arm behind our captive's back.

"You are all so fucking dead," Mikey mumbled and Carter twisted harder until he was rewarded with a pained grunt and then silence. I went first, followed by Mike who had Carter's weight and strength firmly holding him from behind. Amy took the steps gingerly, maybe half afraid that the gun would go off if jostled unwisely. We walked through the small half-finished storage area into the utility room, a small gas furnace, electric water tank, and stacked washer-dryer taking up most of the space. The large blue tarp was waiting for us, edges folded upward adjacent to walls and appliances as if to prevent spills.

"Put him in the middle of the tarp," I said to Carter as I opened the athletic bag with Whatshisname in it. I pulled out the smiling skull before letting both it and the bag drop on the tarp.

Carter let go of his captive's arm as Amy trained the shotgun squarely at his chest.

"Are you sure you don't want to cut him up?" Carter said. "I know where there's a wood chopper." Mike looked from Carter to me. I don't think he appreciated the humour.

"No, this is going to be nowhere near as messy." I picked up a pair of garden gloves from where I had left them earlier and used them to grip the handle of a brand-new hammer that I had left leaning against the wall. It was of those hammers with a five-pound head, good for pounding and crushing. "Take it," I ordered. Amy brought the shotgun up a little higher, clearly implying that if Mikey thought he was going to use the hammer on us, he'd be disappointed.

He looked at the barrel of the shotgun and then at Amy. "Let's everybody be calm with that gun. Remember - safety first."

"We'll worry about any accidents if and when they happen." I stepped back as he gripped the hammer. "Now, smash the bones, all of them, but especially the skull and teeth."

"You are a dipshit if you ..."

"SHUT UP!" Amy commanded. "Do as you're told, asshole! As far as the rest of the world knows, you broke into this house, armed and dangerous. You think we couldn't convince them that you had it coming?" I still don't know if she was playing the part or on the edge of shooting him, but I was a believer at the time. I could only imagine her anger at this man, this creep who had tricked her, abducted her, and imprisoned her for hours in a cold, airless shed, her only hope of rescue linked to me and my relative abilities. Talk about well-justified fear.

"Good thing I have other plans for you," I said, as much to Amy as to Mike. I needed him around a little while longer.

He was tentative with the first few blows. Carter gave him some encouragement. "Feeling a little squeamish, Mikey? Blackmailing and kidnapping not prepare you for this sort of work? We haven't got all night, *chief.* Crush them like you mean it."

The sound of the pounding, now louder and more purposeful, took over the room. Amy stayed focused on pointing the shotgun, but Carter caught my eye and gave me a look as if to say, "WTF?" It was as good a time as any to fill in my friends as well as our enemy.

"When you're all done and cleaned up, you're going to leave this place. We are keeping the bag and the hammer. It has your fingerprints and only your fingerprints on it. For now, your clothes are covered in human bone dust, so you're not going to the cops anytime soon. But let's say you give us any trouble in the future, all we have to do is make sure the cops find the bones and the hammer. They'd link you to their destruction as fast as you can say, 'national crime database.' A cop with a cheesy moustache will show up at your door and take you downtown to answer some questions. 'Gee, Mike,' he'll say, 'Whose bones are these? Look at the broken teeth and skull fragments. And the hammer? Guess whose prints are on it? Look, they're yours, Mike. Now, whyever did you crush these bones? Trying to hide something?'"

"You really are a dipshit," Mike growled. "All it proves is that I did the crushing. No more 'n that." Amy didn't say anything but looked at me kind of like she agreed that I didn't seem to have thought things through.

"That depends on where and when they find them. And on what else they discover when they get a warrant to search the burrow you call home. Who knows, maybe they'll trip over evidence that you killed Gary. We already know they like you for that, don't we? No - you're going to leave here and we're never ever going to see you, hear from you or deal with you again."

"They're gonna know they're your dad's bones, boy! I'll tell 'em and they'll prove it. Little thing called a DNA test."

"I'm willing to risk it if you are. Everyone knows I didn't kill him. Do you think they'll be so sure about you? Especially seeing how you've crushed and hidden the evidence so cleverly."

"There's always your sweet little mommy," he said as he brought the hammer down one final time.

"I think we've taken care of that." I had watched the hammer as it fell on the skull over and over again, convinced that its destructive force was enough to erase whatever evidence there may have been. Evidence that Mom had brained Whatshisname years ago, that she had smashed his head in, whacking him once, twice, maybe three times before pushing him over the edge that night. I had seen it - the skull caved in on the side, the likely reason he never got up, why he never walked out of that forest, why Mom and I were still alive.

"And we get to keep the shotgun," Carter said with a smile.

# Chapter Forty-One
## Some Plans Are Not Clear Until After They Happen

I've always found that preparation and clean-up are always the most time-consuming parts of a job around the house. You have to plan for them. And we had - we had even made up a story to tell people in case something went wrong, a story along the lines of what Amy had said, that Crime-Spree Mikey had barged in making no sense, wielding a shotgun and making bizarre demands. Clean-up was also simple. All we had to do was fold and roll up the tarp.

Weirdly, our guest didn't appear to be anxious to leave and took his sweet time. I began to get suspicious - maybe he was stalling for time. What was going on beneath that pinch-faced exterior, with its Camaro moustache twitching over his stained teeth? Maybe he was figuring a new angle.

As I considered what that might be, I realized there was a danger, a Mom-based danger. If she finished work early, if that's even where she went today, she could show up and force an uncomfortable reckoning. None of this had been sanctioned, none of this could be exposed to the light of anyone's gaze. Mom had demonstrated that she absolutely could not be trusted with the big picture. She might object to both my strategy and tactics.

And she would go nuts.

Parent-related problems aside, Mike's presence here wasn't the only compromising element on my to-do list. While I had a substitute athletic bag, one without my prints on it, I had to get rid of the original as well as the tarp. I shoved one inside the other and stashed them behind the furnace.

As far as I know, they're still there.

Maybe I was getting distracted with all the loose ends, maybe my suspicion of Mike had an ironic twist, that I was not watching him closely enough. I had the bag of remains in my gloved hands as we formed an impromptu, and ultimately fateful line going up the stairs. Amy went up first, taking the shotgun up to cover Mike. I made sure that I was behind him, not wanting Carter to do any more wrestling, grappling, or whacking, despite the fact that he was the only one of us who could match the skinny creep's strength.

Despite being such a loser, Mike clearly did not like losing. He wanted his easy money. He harboured sleazy and entirely unnatural visions of some kind of tryst with She-Who-Gave-Me-Life or Amy or both. He was the sort of person who uses violence to get what he wants and he was definitely not the sort of person who was willing to be bettered and humiliated by a teenager, or even a team of teenagers. He thought he was clever, quick and strong enough to take his weapon from a teenage girl and her two dipshit friends.

That's why he did it. The motivation. The how was all about opportunity.

I'm not sure what sort of mid- to long-term plan his desiccated brain might have come up with, so I imagine he just thought he had to act or suffer the consequences. Like I said, Amy and the shotgun were ahead of him and I was right behind. When we were up the stairs and moving in a line toward the front door he made his move. He thought he could wrestle the shotgun from her and then face us all down once more in order to dictate new and rewarding terms for the future of our relationship.

He was kind of right.

"Chase, there's a car turning into your driveway!" Amy said as she peeked out the small sidelight near the front door.

Mike lunged forward as quick as a cat, seizing the shotgun with both hands. Panicking at my sudden loss of control, I followed, also trying to grab the gun. With a sudden violent step, he knocked me back into Carter. The force of our collision knocked him onto his butt but kept me upright.

Amy, screaming hurtful things about Mike's parents, demonstrated the strength, stamina, and determination of a radically pissed-off woman and she did not give up her grip on the shotgun. Mike tried to lever the gun up, using his greater height to wrench it away from Amy as I dived in to help her pull it down. My left hand was on the barrel and my right was near the trigger.

I can only imagine what images, sensations, impressions were going through Amy's mind during the brief frenetic struggle, what kind of passionate fear or hatred she may have felt, what kind of strength she took from it or what kind of weakness it engendered. I only knew my greatest fear, that she and I were not strong enough, not decisive enough, not resolute enough to finish what we had started.

Only one word came to my mouth. "NOOoooooo!" I wailed. In a confluence of physical purpose, a coincidence of forces applied at just the necessary time and in the necessary direction, Amy pushed while I pulled and the gun came partway free of Mike's grip.

And then the world exploded.

Mike flew backwards with a look of surprise on his face. The force of the gunshot sent him into the wall and then he bounced forward and down, his face to the floor and his eyes open.

I will always remember that. His eyes were still open.

The only sound coming through the ringing in my ears was the sound of Loki barking. My arms fell to my sides and I gazed at the scene with a strange thought swimming up from the deep thought-well of my overwhelmed brain. "How am I gonna get this cleaned up before Mom gets home?"

Carter had not been able to get into the foray and that must have meant that it was brief, that it only seemed to last terrible minutes, because he just kept saying, "Oh, shit. Oh, shit. Oh, shit."

The only sound that came from Amy was her breathing, short, sharp, and shocked.

It turned out that I didn't have to worry, though. About getting it all cleaned up. As I dumbly stood there, the front door burst open and two people came lurching though. Mom and Jason Stone, Amy's dad. I don't remember what they said if they said anything at all. Their faces were mirroring Amy's and probably mine - uncomprehending, appalled amazement. But with no blood spatter.

Amy looked at them and her eyes grew wide.

And then she dropped the gun. And fell to her knees.

# Chapter Forty-Two
## This Time I Know Who the Killer Is

You'd think I'd be getting used to all the police interrogation stuff. I might have but this time it was different. Maybe it was the whole violence part, the part where there was a dead scumbag on the floor in my house and I had to keep my dog from sniffing him. Maybe it was the gore on the walls and the acrid stink of whatever they put in shotgun shells to make them go boom. Maybe it was the lights and sirens and howling dog and traumatized friends and hysterical mother. And maybe it was the whole responsibility thing, where I knew that I had not killed the guy, but that maybe I was responsible for the situation that led to his death.

That part I kept to myself.

After getting a once-over by the paramedics, we were all hauled to the police station downtown and put in separate holding areas. Because I am capable of learning I didn't say much to anyone until She-Whose-Advice-is-Golden, a still uncomfortably pregnant Alexa, showed up. While I think Amy's dad got to sit in on her interview, it was going to be just me and Alexa. Mom couldn't sit in with me because the cops still thought we were maybe in on a serial killing spree together, a mother-and-son killing compact directed against underachieving lowlife losers.

If you think about that even for a moment, you can see how absurd it is - it's a job we could literally NEVER finish.

Alexa and I had a few minutes to confer before the detectives arrived.

"What have you got yourself mixed up in?" she sighed as she sank slowly into her chair.

"It's not me and it's not my friends. It was that psycho guy. He storms in waving a shotgun and carrying that bag of ... whatever it was but he said it was bones ... and he demands to see Mom and she's not there and he went ballistic and he was gonna shoot us and we fought back. I'm sure Amy didn't mean to pull the trigger. It was an accident."

"My goodness, we are goin' to be here for a while, aren't we?" She settled in with a legal pad and pen and slowly took me through my story, at least those parts of it that I could tell her before the detectives arrived.

The door opened and it was my old friend the Great Detective - Reynolds. The expression on his face was all at once annoyed for having been dragged in here late on Halloween night and satisfied that he thought he finally had me where he wanted me. Call it annoyifaction. And the tape rolled and the questions started.

Yup. Met the guy once before to deliver something. (I had to say that - if they were following Mike like Amy said, they already knew.)

Nope - not sure what it was all about - you'll have to ask Mom. (And she would tell the truth, that she was being blackmailed by someone who claimed to have found Whatshisname's bones.)

Yup. We did make a phone call earlier - someone has been making nuisance calls, just hanging up, and I was feeling like getting back at them, so we did. Then someone called back and it must have been him because he made NO sense at all and I hung up. (This was also a story both Amy and Carter were in on. It was Carter's idea in case we had to explain the phone record. I owe him, like, a million favours by now.)

Nope. I didn't let the guy in, the door was unlocked - Halloween, you know. He just burst through and demanded to see Mom and got furious she wasn't there. (A modicum of truth always helps a lie become ...  a better lie.)

No, I don't know what time it was. It was after the little kids were off the street. He had to have been there a while because he got more and more riled and then pulled out the shotgun. (Another self-improving lie.)

What did you expect me to do? We just cooperated. I put the dog in the spare room and we all just waited for Mom to come home.

I don't know what set him off. He just got more and more frustrated, kept going on about some old lady and Gary - yeah, he mentioned Gary, but I don't know what he could have had to do with all this. And then he saw the lights in the driveway, Mom and Mr. Stone coming in. He got excited and started to point his gun at the door and both Amy and I went for him at the same time. We struggled and he was strong. Amy must have pulled the trigger by accident when we pulled the gun away from him.

"Why are you looking at me like that?"

He didn't bother answering, so Alexa filled in the uncomfortable silence.

"My clients seem to be the victims in this situation, detective, do they not? An armed man, one of low repute, I'll wager, enters the home, confines and threatens children. Their actions may have saved their lives as well as the lives of Ms. Martel and Mr. Stone." Alexa tapped her pencil impatiently against her legal pad.

Reynolds just kept staring at me. Finally, he asked the question, the one I could not answer. "What are we going to find when we compare the DNA in those bones in that bag with yours, Chase?"

"I don't know what you're talking about."

"And if he did," Alexa cut in, "I would advise him to let you make your own conclusion once you've done your job. I, for one, look forward to seeing the fruits of a thorough investigation, one in which you will discover the many answers you are searching for. As for the moment, Chase is leaving and I am staying so that you may interview his mother in MY presence, do you understand?"

It's not as though I actually was allowed to leave, but Alexa did have a way of moving things along. Other interviews took place. Amy and Carter would be questioned closely. They would either corroborate my story or they wouldn't. I was left alone in an interrogation room, a little camera in the corner keeping watch.

I remembered what cops said about innocent people - they are often more nervous than the guilty ones. Sometimes the guilty ones even fall asleep. The absolute fact that everyone behaves differently in unfamiliar circumstances means nothing, but I could play it their way, giving them the performance they expected of an innocent person - nervous and stressed out. It wasn't hard - it's not like I was guilty of doing anything except inviting Mikey over to play.

I performed my act for a couple of hours, fidgeting and twitching in my chair, getting up and pacing like a caged tiger I saw in a zoo once. I sat down for about the thirty-fourth time when I heard a loud wail, sort of like a wounded mastodon might have bellowed as it was impaled by neanderthal spears. There were some loud voices and I saw shadows pass by the frosted glass of the door a few times before I heard it again.

Yup. Alexa was in danger of giving birth in the police station.

I don't know what the minions of the justice system had in store for me that night, but Alexa's magic, both deliberate and not, had spectacular consequences. First, there are worse places to go into labour than a police station. At least there are lots of people who are used to dealing with emergencies. And there were paramedics fairly close to take her away to a better place to give birth. A good outcome. A healthy baby girl.

But the spectacular consequence for me, for us, was that our legal counsel had been incapacitated. Even Reynolds could not imagine she was faking it. So, instead of finding us another lawyer, which would take hours and keep everyone up even later, they let us go. We weren't supposed to talk to each other, or at least me and Carter and Amy, but we could leave. I think Mr. Stone used his inside knowledge of the system to whisper in a couple of ears that it didn't make sense for anyone to continue all night long, especially as it was looking like we were victims, not perpetrators.

Sure, we had to come back the next day. But at least we got to go home, or at least in our case to a pet-friendly motel. Our house was a grotesque crime scene, still ghoulishly decorated with Halloween trimmings - severed limbs, skulls, that sort of thing. It would be a few days before we got permission to move back in and clean it up.

Even weirder, after we left, Mom did not grill me. She did not interrogate me and find the obvious, for her, holes in my story, read the obvious, for her, non-verbal cues in my face that would tell her just when and by how much I was bending the truth or violating it entirely. It was as if she had simply accepted my story as she first heard it.

Why would she do that? Was she making the choice not to know what really went down? Or was she afraid that I might have some questions of my own that might have uncomfortable answers? What else was she hiding?

All of that was bouncing around my head the next day. I had kept my mouth shut, kept close all the questions about Whatshisname, about how she'd killed him and then also killed Gary and Don but then couldn't seem to handle Mike. So many nagging, needling, and ultimately necessary questions.

So we went back to be interviewed - twice, and on the second time Murray, our new lawyer dude who I think Alexa chose for us between contractions, put his foot down. We would not be going again. SuperAlexa wouldn't have let it go even that far, but I wasn't faulting Murray.

In response to a different set of questions (I guess they were trying to trip me up, but come on), I gave them the same scenario I had before, the same one I had loudly and clearly given Mom and Mr. Stone as soon as they blundered in. "Mike showed us - these crushed bones - he said they were ... Dad's and he said Gary found them ... wow, Gary, as if we hadn't had enough of him ... And then Mike said he wasn't going to leave without money or jewels. He started to wave around the shotgun and Carter told him to be careful and he just let loose with this racist rant. The guy was losing it. Both Amy and I went for him at the same time, and ... and the gun just went off. I don't know anything about shotguns. I didn't know the safety was off, or if shotguns even have a safety." And I watched Reynolds' moustache twitch and I saw Tremblay's pen tap tap tap on her notebook.

What's more, our new counsel filled us in on Mike's criminal past. He seemed big on aggravated assault and theft - this may have been his first foray into extortion, but his past supported our version of him - a scumbag who wanted to steal from us and hurt us.

When I got back to it, school was weird. People looked at me all the time. It was annoying. A vice-principal talked to me, which wasn't too bad. He was nicer than he appeared when he was trolling the hallways. Wanted to figure out if I needed counselling, if I was traumatized. I had to stop myself from laughing.

When I tried to call Amy the next day, I had to use their landline, as her cell was out of service. I quickly discovered that my social life was, again, limited.

"Oh, hi, Chase," Mr. Stone said as soon as he picked up the phone. "Listen, just for a few days, maybe it's a good idea to not have any contact with Amy or Carter - you don't want to appear conspiratorial to anyone who might be looking for that sort of thing. Nothing personal."

When I complained at home, Mom thought that was good advice. Carter's parents seemed to agree. I remember his dad looking at me closely on Halloween night, not saying anything, probably trying to figure out if I was the victim I said I was or a criminal prodigy who had landed his son in the wrong kind of adventure. The fact that I was kind of both meant I didn't have any trouble looking him in the eye.

After a while, it all got to me. Okay, maybe it was only a couple of days, but one afternoon in those long long hours between school and supper, when Mom was just sitting there reading a book in our budget-priced motel room like there was nothing wrong in the world, I brought it up. I needed her to ask me what had really happened. So that I could lie to her face and be done with it.

"Gee, I guess he got his dates mixed up."

"What?"

"Mike - he must have got his dates mixed up."

"What do you mean?"

"You'd arranged another exchange, right? Wasn't he coming sometime to score Mrs. Leckey's jewellery? I know you couldn't tell the cops that."

"I did not ... steal her jewellery."

"But there had to be a reason. You know, for him to show up like that."

"I thought you probably invited him over."

"Me? Are you nuts?"

"I don't know. Are you?"

I think it was her way of telling me that she suspected I had lured Mike over, an act that shouted out to the world that I was indeed a dipshit. But she didn't pursue it and that was really REALLY strange. I figured it out later. It had nothing to do with me and everything to do with Amy.

Amy, with the eyes and clavicles, and talent.

Amy, who was the other killer in my life.

Killer. Not murderer.

# Chapter Forty-Three

## Be Grateful for the Parents You Don't Have

A few days went by and we were allowed back into our house. Mom hired professionals to clean up the gore. It would be up to us to fill holes and paint. And I was glad to see the garden gloves there and not in an evidence bag. They were useful.

There was only one last issue that had to be resolved with the cops, one last question they were sure to have. I had rehearsed the scenario.

"Those remains - did you know they were your father's?" Detective Reynolds would ask.

"What's that?" I'd say. Reynolds would just stare at me, like he did, as if it worked. "My father's? How ... could ... that be?" I planned on pausing here, searching for comprehension and finding only outrage. "That bastard! Did he kill my father?" I would jump to my feet, demanding answers, wanting to know why people like Mike Lawrence were allowed to wander the streets alongside decent folk. The humanity. The incompetence! Stuff like that.

Never happened. The question didn't come.

Days went by before we learned the truth.

But the truth did not set me free - it made me go sideways.

Whatshisname was not my father.

My new lawyer, MurrayMan, told me - not in so many words, of course. He just said that there was no match, that the remains had not been identified. Since the police had my DNA, that had to mean he wasn't my father.

And there was no possible identification from dental records. Turns out Whatshisname wasn't big on dentists and Mike had done a fair job smashing his teeth up anyway.

I had his last name, sure, but that's all I had of his.

How did that make me feel? First, relieved that I didn't have any psycho-killer DNA. At least not from the Y chromosome. My father had NOT tried to kill me. Maybe he thought he was my father, of course. Maybe Mom did, too. Then again, maybe neither of them knew.

This train of thought sucked out loud. Did Mom know who my biological father is? Did he, I mean the guy, dear ol' genetic progenitor, or whatever I should call him, did *he* know *he* had an awkward seventeen-year-old son? Whatshisname had been dead for a long time, and I had got used to the idea that whatever "father" I might have had was dead and gone and good riddance. But now everything was different.

Mom had been lying to me all these years.

Why would she tell me that my father had hit her if she knew he wasn't my father?

So, taking one killing at a time, we had to talk. Saturday seemed a good day, a nice happy day off to help us talk about just who had killed whom. We were both at home. Loki was fed, watered, and walked. Laundry was making its rumbling and whirring noises in the basement. The white noise and safe environment seemed a perfect context for me to bring up the herd of elephants in the kitchen.

These awkward little mother-son talks were getting tiresome, I shit you not.

"Robinson," she began, "it was complicated ..."

"And?" I asked when her pause showed no sign of ending.

"David Robinson and I were married after I found out I was pregnant with you. He always knew that it was likely that you were not his biological son. It made everything worse for him ... that there was doubt. You were a walking, talking reminder that I had another relationship just before him. It's one of the reasons that I made sure you had his surname, so that he might bond with you. I said we should just do a paternity test, but he found that idea somehow terrifying, like his humiliation would be complete if it turned out that you were not his.

"It was a stupid idea getting married but he said all the right things, promised to look after me, after us, and I was feeling vulnerable and alone. Your grandparents knew that I had married him on the rebound even though I'd known him for a couple of years. They never liked him, never had any confidence in our relationship, which didn't help anything."

"Was that why he went all murdery on us? Is that why he was going to kill us in the woods?"

"Maybe ... hard to say exactly."

I *so* wanted to ask her right then and there - did she bash him in the skull oncetwice*three* times? I wanted to know, just so I could say, "Way to go, MOM!" But she still didn't know that I knew she had, did not know that I had seen the evidence, seen the bashed-in braincase. I had to let it go.

"So - who is it then?"

"Who is what?"

"MOM! Come on!"

"You can't ask me that!" Mom shouted at me for the first time ever. "I know it's your business, I understand you deserve to know but I can't tell you! It's way more complicated than you could possibly realize and I have to think about it!"

"How long do you need? Hasn't seventeen years been enough?"

And she just left. Just got up and left. Left the room, left the house with a kind of finality like she didn't know when she was coming back.

So maybe I was being harsh, but it was ME we were talking about, who I am, who I might become, and I might have a walking talking father out there somewhere. I had to talk to someone, share the news, the load, the anxiety. Not Carter. He'd just laugh at me.

So, I texted her. I thought enough time had elapsed, that maybe we could talk face to face.

**Me:** Got your phone back?

**Amy:** No. Are you sleeping?

**Me:** Yes.

Okay, texting someone that question was stupid and Amy found a way to make sure I knew. Still, it was a start. We arranged to meet. She wouldn't come to my place, because, well, she killed someone in a horrible shooting incident there, so, you know. I went to her place, where we were blessed with a parent-free environment, her dad having disappeared a couple of hours before.

She opened the front door for me and gave me a small smile. I felt, I don't know, I can only say truly *happy* and reached forward to hug her. While she didn't pull away, she wasn't in a hugging mood, I could tell. I took off my shoes and jacket and followed her into the living room. There I got to sit and gaze around, trying not to be envious of a house that was … just a lot nicer than mine. It was all open concept and minimalistic without being pretentiously Nordic. There was a very cool spiral staircase that rose to a balcony and from there you could get to the rooms, the bedrooms on the second floor if you wanted, but I think it was mostly for show. It always caught my eye – a spiralling journey upward. Yes, I know stairs go in both directions, but it was the journey up that I thought about.

"I have another stupid question," I said, coming back to earth. "Are you okay?"

"I've been better." She slumped into an armchair. I sat on the couch across from her.

"That's a low standard." Silence. I started babbling to fill the void. "The house is almost back to normal. Just have a little painting to do."

"Uh huh."

"So … did your dad tell you? The news? About Whatshisname's bones?"

"Yeah - they're officially unidentified."

"So - you know what that means? I might have a father!"

"I'm sure you've always had a father."

"You know what I mean, a real live father, one who doesn't want to kill me."

"That's only because he hasn't met you."

"Burn. Good one. But you have to see - this is great! You've got no idea what it felt like, to know that my father was a psycho-killer, especially knowing that Mom has her own issues that way. I was beginning to think that I was doomed to struggle against burgeoning homicidal tendencies my whole life."

"And we both know you're not winning that particular battle." She drew her legs up onto the chair and hugged her knees. That distracted me because I have always thought that her knees look sexy good in jeans. But I should have asked her what she meant by that. Seems to me I had very successfully resisted my altogether relatable urge to kill Mikey. She was the trigger-woman. She was the one who'd killed someone, not me.

It was a good thing that I had never told the cops about Mike abducting her, keeping her locked up in a chilled shack. They might have considered her motives for shooting that douchebag to be rock-solid. Not that anyone would have blamed her, but judges could get sticky about these kinds of things. The happiness I was feeling, though, meant that I could overlook any number of cutting remarks, witty barbs and verbal jabs from Amy this afternoon. Things were finally going my way and I could be big about things.

As I took a few seconds for those thoughts to filter through my brain, we were surprised by the sound of the front door opening. And we heard not one but two voices in the front foyer. One of them was definitely Amy's dad, and the other gave me that panicky feeling in my stomach I get when I think I've forgotten to go to a final exam.

It was Mom. As she recognized both voices Amy turned around to look at the hallway our parents would emerge from.

"Oh, you're both here," Jason Stone said. "That's just as well."

I was too surprised, if not slightly horrified, to manage speech. It got worse a second or two later.

"We have something to tell you," Mom said.

Something to ...? She's coming into Amy's house with Amy's dad after storming out when I demanded to know who my father is. And *they* have something to tell us?

The couch beneath my butt lost molecular cohesion as my vision began to fade to black. I plunged, unable to breathe, into a maelstrom of chaos, confusion, and terror, a precognitive wasteland of despair, an abyss of misery.

Okay, I fainted.

# Chapter Forty-Four

## All the Best Misery Begins with Joy

"What is the *matter* with you?"

I wasn't sure who said that. I swam out of my lightless chasm with a paper bag over my mouth. I guess I must have started to hyperventilate. Held by Mom, the bag slowly collapsed and refilled in front of my face as I watched in dumb stupefaction. I reached up and removed her hand from the bag and took it in my own fist as I sat up. Then, as another wave of panic set in, I put my head between my knees, bringing the bag up to my mouth once more.

"Does this happen often?" Jason Stone asked.

"No," Amy and Mom said together.

"Is he sick?"

"No," they chorused. And then looked at each other instead of at me.

I let go of the bag and croaked from between my knees, "Sorry - just a lot going on, you know?" I slowly brought my head up to see the three of them regarding me with various mixtures of concern, annoyance and disbelief.

"So, what is it? What do you have to tell us? Don't worry about me. I can handle the truth." I suddenly felt stronger, that it was time to face up to life, and then maybe enter a fugue state for a month or two. But not here, not right now. Later.

"It's about who your father is," Mom said.

"Yeah, I guessed that."

"It's someone you know."

"Uh huh. Yeah."

Here it comes. I'll hold my breath and I won't fall over. I will be scarred for life, but I will survive. Jason must be my dad. They're going to tell me that Amy's my half-sister. It's an old story, often told. It didn't make it any easier.

And in my heart of hearts, I know that Luke Skywalker never felt the kind of pain that I was feeling.

"Well, not someone you've ever met, I guess," Mom said.

What?

"Jason had an older brother, Ryan."

What?

"He and your mom were what you could call an item," Mr. Stone said. "He died in a car accident more than seventeen years ago. It was devastating. Nothing was ever the same."

"Wait a minute," Amy cut in. "Are you two saying that Uncle Ryan is … was … Chase's father?"

"That's what we're saying, yes," Mr. Stone said quickly, sparing Mom the expense of saying it.

"And there are some interesting implications for you," he said looking me in the eye.

Yeah, seriously. Amy and I were cousins. That *could* be totally creepy.

"My mother, Amy's grandmother, was a wealthy woman when she died. In her will, there was a provision for Ryan and any children he might have had. It was never taken out, so it's likely that it's legally binding. You may be eligible for an inheritance. It'll be complicated, but we can work it out. We may need a DNA test, though. We can just compare yours to mine to see if we're in the same family."

And it dawned on me that this was the complication. One of several. Other people, their memories, their relationships, and even their bank accounts were caught up in our family drama.

"Say something, Chase," Mom said gently.

"It … I … we …"

Mr. Stone took mercy on me. "It's a lot to take in. To find out that the man who you thought was your father isn't. To discover that you might have a very different sort of relationship open to you. And then to have it taken away. I'd probably faint, too."

Amy was unimpressed. "Chase passed out just when you walked through the door. A premature keeler-over."

"Thanks," I said as both Mom and Amy's dad tried not to laugh.

# Chapter Forty-Five
## Existence Is a Fatal Condition

There was more. Painfully more. Mom and Jason Stone had been seeing each other, on and off, for a while. The new revelation made no difference to them, of course. Mom had no compunction about dating the man whose daughter was the niece of an old boyfriend.

Carter loved being right. The only word I can think of to describe his behaviour is trying. Every time he saw either one of us, he'd say, "Hi cuz!" Both Amy and I wanted to smack him. He was smug and happy and delighted to watch Amy and me squirm and cringe, to force our brains to accommodate a new reality.

Rich was more sympathetic but only a little. I guess because he had a girlfriend and didn't want to be her cousin. In his head, or more like on it, he had his own problems. He had to cut off his dreads because Émilie's granny didn't understand them and he got tired of answering her questions. For him, it seemed as traumatic as what the rest of us had been through.

The ordeal of cutting his hair did not compare to the injustice of my very existence. The whole thing made me want to shout that I HAD DIBS! I was totally there in that family first, sort of. I guess Mom was, but that's not fair, I wasn't even alive yet and Mom was interested in the other guy, in Ryan the older brother. In … Dad.

Who was then quickly killed in a car crash and Mom got scooped up by Whatshisname.

My very existence seems to carry with it a significant danger to all men associated with Mom, doesn't it?

The worst is when some addled adult says, "How does it feel to be cousins?" Both Amy and I wanted to melt, she out of embarrassment that no matter what she did, she'd still be related to me. Me, I melted because my longstanding infatuation with her might appear kinda awkward, mildly improper, and definitely creepy. And that's just the way family and friends might feel.

Doubly creepy would be if Mom and Jason had a long-term relationship, if we had to move in together. I would feel like we were in a reality TV show called *Chasing Amy* full of mini-dramas just before the commercials and cliffhanger break-ups at the end of the season. Our family would become a crass punchline.

I had to outlast Mom, make sure she didn't make any bad moves. It was a waiting game I thought I could win. Her history with men was consistent. They didn't last long. Most of them seemed to die relatively young. Amy's dad is different, though. He is not a loser. And his presence in Mom's life is the only thing that explains why she is not in jail for something. He must have at least given advice on how to deal with Mikey, or what to say about Whatshisname's remains. Maybe she'd talked with SuperAlexa or Murraydude the lawyer, I don't know.

I might have to hang in there for years, on standby. That's where my original Plan was brilliant. If she just hooked up with some older rich dude who was about to bite the big one anyway, everyone would be happy. Except maybe her. Jason Stone seemed fit and healthy. Not a big drinker. Didn't skydive or anything useful like that. Wait - he did go rock climbing. But it's not like I wished bad things for him, it was just that I would have preferred if he didn't date my mother.

My mind came back to this place often. It was a decision point, a divide, a fork in the road that stopped me in my tracks. I couldn't possibly get rid of him creatively, as then I would be risking my relationship with Amy. If I just let everything go, though, I was risking exactly the same thing.

I coped by releasing a little creative energy. I was considering revisiting my animated feature project, long neglected because of recent events. The sticking point was always my protagonist and what response anyone could possibly have to a world full of low-level predators and parasites, a response that didn't require a superpower. I wondered if the cause rather than the behaviour itself might be addressed, if the main character might seek solace in taking revenge on the biggest parasites of them all. The parasites that have become predators because of their lust for profit, power, influence and control.

Yes, I mean the big social media companies that want you to devote your life to *them*. To enhancing their ability to manage your access to information, your human relationships, and your bank account.

I brought it up with Amy. I dropped in on her at home one day when I knew Mom and Jason were out together. I never used to show up unannounced, but now I felt sort of entitled. She said Hi and let me in as if she'd invited me. I told her we needed to talk and she agreed. But I wanted to talk movie-making magic.

"Wait a sec," she said after I shared my latest idea, "you're going after big media now. Before you were just dealing with oblivious losers. What's one cranky cartoon character going to do against social media behemoths?"

"Animated, not cartoon," I objected. "And that - the online world - is where people learn to devalue everything but their own little headspace. That's the point - she'll figure out how to help people discover parasitism in their lives and they'll do the rest. They have to know themselves, to understand why they do things, why they devalue in-person human interaction. A social revolution."

"She?"

"Yup - taking the plunge."

"And *you* are gonna tell *other people* that they should get to know themselves better."

"Yeah. Why not?

"Why not take the first step yourself. Why not go all the way?"

"Go all the way where?"

"To reality. Give up this absurd animation thing. You can't even draw with a computer program telling you what to do! Just write something - I don't know, a short story, a novel, a screenplay if you like, but stop deluding yourself. No idea like *this* is gonna make an animated feature."

That was harsh, but not unprecedented. I countered with an old tactic.

"Because words are your thing doesn't mean they're mine."

"They're *completely* your thing. You just don't want to see it. Like you don't want to see a lot of things."

"I don't know what you're talking about." And neither did she, of course.

"You should see yourself, for once. You think you're some gawky, geeky animation club nerd. But look at who your parents are and then look at yourself. My Uncle Ryan was dead handsome, and even your friends know your mom's hot. You're smart, you're good-looking, and you write way better than you'll ever be able to draw. Your biggest issue is that you don't get YOU."

"I get me - I'm nobody. Skinny, crooked teeth with both bad hair and a bad haircut. I'm cinematic, not verbal, and I'm totally transparent."

"See - you don't even understand what you're good at. It's a little disturbing. You have some fairly specific talents, the kind that makes me want to say something before you exercise them once again."

"Say something? Go ahead." There was a pause while I held her eyes in mine for a few seconds. Then, she let me have it.

"You are NOT going to go all Hamlet-y on my dad."

"What are you talking about?"

"You know what I mean - the uncle gets together with Hamlet's mother? Hamlet kills him?"

"Whoa - spoiler alert!"

She didn't buy it and kept looking at me as if she was seriously intimating that I might be considering killing her dad. I decided to sidestep that particular outrage.

"Me? I'd be more worried about Mom. She's the killer. Several times over."

She looked at me again for five uneasy seconds. Then she sat up straight in her chair, crossed her arms and crossed her legs. In her jeans. Which distracted me a bit.

"Your *mom's* the killer?"

"Right. We know she bashed Whatshisname's head in. He had it coming."

"No, we don't. It probably happened just the way she said. Your imagination came up with the head-bashing stuff, and you made sure no one could ever know for sure when you decided to make Mike crush the skull. It makes me wonder what you made up about Gary."

"Nothing - I made up nothing about Gary. He gave Mom about a hundred reasons to end him."

"Are you actually saying that SHE did it, that your mother planted doctored eye drops on Gary Twolan, so that he would inadvertently kill himself as soon as he'd had a rough night and needed to get the red out?"

"Well, I don't know for sure ..."

"Yes you do."

"How do you figure that?"

"Because you're the one who did it. You gave him those eye drops."

"I wish."

"You hated him more than she did."

"To know him was to hate him."

"It was clever the way you wiped all the prints off just that one item, the little bottle of eye drops, leaving them on everything else. It introduced just enough ambiguity that, in a city filled with people who hated Gary Twolan, you no longer looked to be the only suspect."

"The universe itself took a deep breath when that guy died."

"And Big Don? No mystery there. You saw your whole life disappearing - again. Your precious Plan in disarray just as you had managed to get it back on track. You're the guy in the hoodie and hat that the cops were looking for. You pushed him. You must have got rid of the clothes in some faraway garbage bin. The only reason that the cops didn't figure you for it was that they were so fixed on your mother."

"Big Don probably tripped and fell. Mom was nowhere near the place."

"I know that - I said it was YOU who pushed him. Maybe after killing Gary, Don wasn't so hard."

"Don was a parasite in Runderwear."

"Maybe you didn't mean to kill him but just that one time you didn't have a proper plan and your temper got the better of you. I'm giving you the benefit of the doubt about Don, trust me, especially because his death was not in your interest. You had no way to get your mom's money back and you lashed out. You gave him a shove and he lost his balance and that was that.

"That's why your final act was so brilliant. No tolerance for error. You lured Mike over. You knew he'd bring his shotgun. You probably did research to make sure you knew how to use it. When you'd got him to do just enough to incriminate himself, you killed him. And I helped. And Carter helped."

"You had your hands on the gun. We struggled - *together* - against that slimeball."

"But why did you insist that I take the shotgun? Carter was by far the better choice. Why did you arrange it so that I would go ahead of him and not behind? It's because you wanted him to do what he did. You planned it that way. And we both know who pulled the trigger."

"*You* did."

"My finger was nowhere near the trigger. Not ever. I was too afraid of it."

"So it was an accident, sure."

"No - you made a decision. He wasn't part of your Plan. And there was no way he was going to walk out of your life that night. He'd be back on his terms and it would be ugly. You must have seen that in his eyes, you must have simply figured it out in that way of yours - he had to die just like Gary did. Just like Don. Like Whatshisname all those years ago. Carter and I were involved just enough so that we'd lie for you out of self-preservation if not friendship. And just like Gary, Mike was such a lowlife that nobody was going to shed a tear, ask too many questions.

"But how did you know your mom and my dad were going to come up the walk at that time? Just in time to see me with the gun standing over Mike's dead body? Could you have planned it, timed it so precisely? If that's so, you are an evil genius, Chase Robinson."

My ears were burning. My palms sweating. My heart made an unpleasant pounding in my chest and neck. Was I an evil genius? AM I an evil genius?

"Just admit it to yourself, that's all I ask. If Chase lies to Chase and more, convinces Chase that he was just a spectator while all of this went on, Chase is lost. Not just an evil genius. A monster."

Gary. Which was the bigger risk to me, Mom, The Plan - Gary dead or Gary alive - was hard to decide. I knew he had an EpiPen. So did Mom. Who knew that the guy would be so stupid? If he'd just jabbed himself, or told whoever he was living with to do it, he'd still be stinking up the landscape.

Don was a blur. My confrontation with him at Rideau Station. Did that really happen? I remember the running, the fear, the sirens. Not the push. I don't remember the scornful look on his face, the feel of my hands on his chest, the same feeling that Mom probably had when she pushed Whatshisname over that cliff. And I'm sure I don't recall the face of the driver looking with horror down on Don, not at me.

We all knew that I had planned Mike's visit. But the struggle with the shotgun was different. I couldn't have known he was going to make a move for it, I couldn't have known who was going to burst through the door just after the gun went off.

That means I'm not an evil genius, right?

And so, I couldn't be a monster either.

Maybe Amy was just in denial. About pulling the trigger. Couldn't handle what she'd done.

I looked in her eyes. There in the deep green eyescape was my own ugly face. What did she call me? Good-looking? Who's deluding themselves now?

Amy was losing it.

# Chapter Forty-Six
## Three Points of Contact

If I look up and crane my neck back just a little, I see something truly magnificent - a blue sky in November. If I look forward, I see only rock, only cliff. Behind me, I know, is distance. Nothing but space. Not good for someone who has more than an average fear of heights.

I extend my right hand and clamp my carabiner onto an anchor. I'm told it's actually called a quickdraw, but the point is that I have a harness attached to a gizmo secured to an anchor so that I do not kill myself climbing this bit of the Eardly Escarpment. I pause to take stock and plan the next bit of my ascent, but I am having trouble staying focused.

Three points of contact, I keep thinking.

The first point - Amy. She has some issues. I overlook them because she's so worth it. One of her quirks is that once she arrives at a conclusion it's hard to change her mind. I am going to have a time convincing her that I am neither evil nor a genius. I know what I am. The good-looking thing was just weird and the idea that I can write defies all logic.

While I hang off a rock face, Amy is hanging with some friends. Not BOB. What a loser. He got the boot because he was all bent out of shape that she didn't reply to all his texts. I've been deleting them whenever Amy's out of the room.

Even without BOB around, there has been a chill between us. Maybe she truly thinks I am a monster. Or maybe she just doesn't want me in her family screwing things up. From her point of view, she has to share both her dad and her inheritance with me and Mom.

Right now, I am sharing this cliff with her dad, who is doing his best to see that I survive. Fresh air, late autumn sunshine. No She-Who-Gave-Me-Life, no cops, no criminal elements. Just the two of us, me and Amy's dad.

Mom's boyfriend.

The second point of contact.

My mind pictures the DNA test kit we got from a lab in Toronto. I dutifully followed the instructions and packed up the samples to be sent away. They are waiting for me in my room to get sent by courier. I plan to do that when I get back.

Two sets of samples.

I made sure to get an extra kit.

One set will likely show what we think it will, that I am related to Jason Stone, and that, therefore, Ryan Stone was my father. I'd get an inheritance. I could pay tuition.

The Plan unfolds as it should.

The other set of samples will show that I am not.

If a genetic analyst looked closely at that second set, they might find that I have Indigenous roots, that I am related to the Anishinaabe people of the region. It's a very particular profile. That's what Carter told me as he proudly contributed some cheek cells on a cotton-tipped stick. I have to remember to stay friends with that guy. He knows ALL my secrets.

More careful climbing, more shouted encouragement as we go from anchor to anchor. While we are alone today, it's a route taken by many people many times before. No surprises.

Third point of contact. Mom. We are already at a point where she doesn't trust me very much. If I fiddled with the DNA tests, there would be a big surprise if not a total shock waiting for her. If I am not related to the Stone family, she might freak.

I had it covered.

"No, I am NOT having my DNA tested again! I don't CARE who BIODAD is - I just want to get on with my life!" Put out a little self-involved teenage angst and some amygdala-based decision-making and I'd be okay.

As for Mom, I know that I have to keep my eye on her, on what she does, on the choices she makes. Jason Stone seems a good choice - maybe the fact that he is not a loser would fog her brain with happy relationship-gap-decreasing chemicals.

So, the shock to Mom is a risk I have to take. I will no longer be related to Amy. Not her creepy cousin anymore. She will get her family back and maybe that distance would help her see that I am not the monster she thinks I am. And I'll get none of her inheritance. No danger of that kind of resentment.

Give her some time and Amy will probably get over the bizarre idea that I might go Hamlet-y on her dad. Like I told her, she has more to fear from Mom. She's the one who kills the men in her life. I can't help it if I have a killer pedigree.

Besides, the comparison is all wrong. Jason Stone didn't kill my dad and then marry my mother like Hamlet's Uncle Claudius. And if one more man associated with my mother ends up dead, there will be no end to Detective Reynolds' questions and moustache twitching. Besides, Amy's dad is not a parasite or a predator. He won't be pissing Mom off in that please-kill-me kinda way that the others had. Still, if Jason Stone weren't around, that might clear the decks for me in a number of ways.

Wait a minute - maybe Amy meant Polonius, Ophelia's father, killed - accidentally on purpose? Hamlet just expressing his noble sword-wearing privilege.

"Is everything okay?" Amy's dad shouted at me from his position just below me. I think he could have been up and down the cliff three or four times by now if it weren't for babysitting me.

"Yeah, no problem, just resting my muscles a bit so that they don't cramp!"

I'm not sure how happy Jason Stone is that I am the son of the woman he's dating, or that I might be his blood relative, or that I am obviously attached to his daughter. In his head, I'm the one who nearly got Amy killed. He knows the police suspected me of killing Gary. I must have not three but *four* strikes against me. If I were no longer a blood relative, what would that do to his willingness to tolerate me?

If you think about it, I should be careful that he doesn't throw ME off a cliff.

Bad joke. This is not the time to think about anybody falling off of anything. It's like riding a bike and trying *not* to hit a lamp post. You're toast.

Getting closer to the top, paying strict attention to my instructions, but with some room in my head to notice, I am stunned by the cinematic potential of rock climbing. I lift myself clear of the last handholds, use my legs for one final boost, and I am there, at the top, looking out over the Ottawa River Valley, trees fading from their autumn glory, but still a satisfying colour palette to contrast with the rich blue sky. Jason Stone rises over the lip of the cliff, much more confident and efficient than I.

They say that, subconsciously, people who are afraid of heights want to kill themselves - or someone else, I'll bet. Imagining themselves giving in to the desire is what makes them afraid.

But the view up there, the exercise, the air, they give me a sense of clarity.

The Plan is a construct. I can make a new Plan.

Amy Stone is a person. There is only one Amy.

The first phase of The New Plan will feature the rejuvenation of my relationship with Amy, a relationship of choice, not blood. The way it used to be.

The rest of it, my current unemployment and impoverished tuition-less existence, my life after high school, Mom's problem with killing, all of that I will figure out.

I could start with my reality gap. Maybe I have to learn how to do unpleasant things today in order to have a satisfying life tomorrow. Remove obstacles, make an effort.

I could start today. NOW, today.

Gap-reduction. Obstacle-elimination.

*Mom's new boyfriend*, I muse as I step toward Amy's dad to give him a congratulatory high-five as we look over the valley.

And then, the unthinkable.

A slip, a panicked grab.

Disbelieving, accusing eyes receding. He falls as if in slow motion, bounces once, twice.

Stillness.

"Ready to head back down?" His voice breaks into my head, brings me back. "It can be a lot harder than going up. Remember your three points of contact. Planning is vital."

"Sounds good," I say.

No one needs to tell me about planning.

And, like someone said, safety first.

The End

# Acknowledgements

Thanks to my wife Denise, who let me quit my day job.

Thanks to Colleen Osiowy, line editor and beta reader, and sister-in-law, for all her time and hard work and feedback in what must have seemed an endless stream of emails.

Thanks to Jeff May for artistic digital gimcrackery (cover design).

I also really appreciated being able to use the web site of the Mississauga of the Credit First Nation for the lesson in Anishnaabemowin. Miigwech.

# About the Author

A career that spanned decades as well as continents was all it took to encourage Dave Smith to give up the jet-setting lifestyle of a high school teacher for the fame, glamour, and piles of cash of the independent author.

Raised and educated in Saskatchewan, he now lives in Ottawa and spends much of the day hammering away on his wireless keyboard, sometimes walking a loud-mouthed Beagle, and always taking care of family.

If you enjoyed this, please rate it on the seller's website.
See www.onlydavesmith.com for other  soon-to-be-released works by Dave Smith.
@onlydavesmith is where you can see pictures of my dog.

Dave Smith is not a clever pseudonym.